Okinawa Moon

by

Arthur C. Oroz

This is a work of fiction. The events and characters described herein are imaginary and are not intended to refer to specific places or living persons. Some events and activities depicted in this book did occur during the Korean War, but have been treated with literary license.

OKINAWA MOON
All Rights Reserved
Copyright © 2013 by Arthur C. Oroz

DEDICATION

This book is dedicated to my four beautiful daughters:
Laura, Diane, Michelle and Gina

ACKNOWLEDGEMENT

This book would not have been published if not for the encouragement, persistence and action by my lovely wife, Joyce.

I also give thanks to our good friend, Tomiko Edmiston, for her assistance, additional editing and expertise in putting this book together.

Chapter 1

Guam

Airman 2nd Class John Montez was tired but couldn't sleep. The island weather, as usual, exuded steam and heat. His bunk, wet with heavy moisture, glued him to the sheet. He looked at the half-naked bodies of his buddies glistening with sweat, their hair matted to their skulls and their chests pumping for air. The airman would doze off for a moment and wake, gasping for breath. The barracks was a steam room with no door, no escape. He knew there was no use wetting a towel and putting it on his body. It would immediately become hot and steamy adding to his misery. The worst part was that he couldn't get up and do something about it—he was going to be here for at least another year unless they carried him out in a box.

Montez croaked to a fellow sufferer in the next bunk, "I don't know how long I can take this!"

"Don't think about it," he replied. "I close my

eyes and see little streams of rushing water in the snow in Maine."

Montez tried to visualize a picture of coolness. It didn't work. Most of his life had been spent in the hot country of the open Southern California's San Joaquin Valley — dry heat, bearable heat, with swamp coolers to give respite. As he sloshed in his bunk, the only cool thing he could think of was an ice-cold beer from the PX. He visualized buying two beers, one to put on the back of his neck and the other to drink slowly, allowing the frosty cold liquid to refrigerate his body.

It happened. The thought of the local slop-chute, The Lair, with its scratchy music and icy beer, took Montez away from the present to that place of cool repose and honorable discourse. The smell of stale beer and echoes of old ballads gave the place a sense of history and purpose. It almost made up for the hot glare of the angry sun, the brief, but incessant emptying of wet vapor, and the steamy aftermath of that pouring.

Montez's buddy, Edwards, a lanky six-foot six-inch Tennessean, liked to say, "A few beers, a good fight and a bad woman were all a man had a God-given right to expect in life."

He slowly dozed off again thinking that at least they had the first, and Edwards would strive mightily for the rest.

Stationed in Guam, the main island of the Mariana Island group for six months, Montez was angry with himself for not enlisting in the

Marines like most of his friends and relatives did. The Air Force promised to send him to aerial photography school. The Marines promised infantry training and how to be a real man. Hell, he figured he didn't need to be a real man. He was in enough trouble already. Still Montez felt that he should have joined a tough outfit like the Marines with their well-known esprit de corp. Air Force basic training was a joke. Hell, he walked farther as a Boy Scout in the hills around the South Central California Valley where he grew up.

Aircraft and Engine Mechanic School in Wichita Falls, Texas, was exactly what he didn't want. Montez wanted to get away from engines, grease and dirt. All his young life had been spent working with his father on cars and working in the fields picking tomatoes, bell peppers and anything else available for a little money. So much for government promises. The training and the inevitable waiting after graduating for something to occur lasted for nearly a year. To add insult to injury, they sent Montez for more schooling at another air base. Finally, they put him on a Liberty ship that headed to the island of Guam. He bobbed across the Pacific Ocean for nearly three weeks, sick as a dog and angry at himself for not joining the Marines — at least they're tough and don't have to go to school all of the time.

Edwards finally put it all in place. "Quit yore bitching 'bout school an such, boy. This here U.S.

Air Force runs on brains, not brawn."

It was exciting, finally reaching the island and smelling the rich, fecund odor coming from the vegetation on the fertile land mass. Even before disembarking from the ship, it hit Montez — hot, humid weather that had him gasping for air, and his uniform was wet with sweat in a few minutes. The harbor was full of working sailors and some Marines. The sailors were working large noisy cranes in huge ships, some taking out and others putting in cargo. The dock area was fascinating to watch from the ship's deck; but Montez, along with other sweaty troops, was ordered to disembark. It was then that he finally came to terms with joining the Air Force. The Marines were stuck over here too and looked as unhappy as everyone else.

The long, hot bumpy drive in what looked like a converted cattle car took the airmen to Andersen Air Force Base on the northern half of the Island. The trip was an education in itself. From the bouncing trailer, Montez could see how the native Chamorros, or Guamanians, lived. Even though the natives were working hard in the sun on their little plots of land, he noted that they weren't sweating. He figured he could get used to the climate as well.

He didn't get used to it. In fact, it got worse. The aircraft mechanics and other ground support personnel were working on B-29 bombers which made up the 19th Bomb Group, Far East Air Forces, in the full glare of the burning sun every day. There were no trees or shade on the flight line except under a wing. On the other hand, when his crew could get leave, their time was spent chugging beer on the beach at Tumon Bay or prowling the island in hope of meeting a girl. Tumon Bay was the most beautiful spot in the world with its white sand and palm trees bending gently to kiss the softly lapping, clear water. When Montez had time between beers, he went swimming in the coral-ringed bay.

Staff Sergeant Gomez, a former Golden Gloves welterweight champ and current sheet metal specialist, summed up Tumon Bay by quietly telling Montez, "Sometimes I feel like crying like a baby when I watch the sun setting. It's beautiful. Heaven must be like this."

The Staff Sergeant turned and looked at Montez; then raising his fist said, "You mention what I said to anyone, cabron, and you're dog meat."

Montez looked at the sergeant's muscled arm and was suddenly very happy he was smiling. At six feet, he had at least three inches on the boxer, but he knew that the sergeant could take him. Montez was very conscious of his age and lack of girth. Everyone was older than his twenty years; even his buddy Edwards was twenty-one years old. To add insult to injury, Montez had the face of a fourteen year old, unlined fair skin tanned by the unrelenting sun, and somewhat sad brown-green eyes, which thwarted his immediate goal of looking a little ferocious or at least sophisticated. He disliked his one prominent feature, a thrusting, slightly hooked-at-the-end nose. Airman 2nd Class Montez didn't know that it would all come together in the near future, and he would have no trouble with the opposite sex. As of now, however, he just knew he looked like a skinny scarecrow and no self-respecting girl would associate with him.

Guam was a piece of paradise, despite its sweltering heat, especially when the sun set in the colored ocean, fusing reds and yellows and purples, as well as other colors that Montez couldn't describe. He felt the heaviness of the painted ocean as the sun slowly submerged into the deep. Moving as it was, it was also a lonely scene. Days and nights, then weeks and months passed tediously for him in paradise with the wearisome sameness that brought a languor to his body and slackness to his mind.

Wading in Tumon Bay one day, the inevitable beer in hand, Montez heard a loudspeaker blurring unintelligible words some distance away. The noise got louder every moment. Suddenly a large military truck broke through the palm trees and brush, loudspeaker blaring, "All military personnel report to your duty station. This is not a drill!"

When the driver saw the drunken group, he stopped the truck and an Army sergeant motioned them forward. The Air Force, Marine and Navy personnel didn't, of course. The sergeant was Army. However, an Army type among them walked to the sergeant and, after a couple of minutes, returned to the group of GIs.

"Looks like we're at war with Korea!" he exclaimed excitedly. "Don't know anything else. That's all he said. Air Force and Navy trucks will be coming to pick up ya'll."

The Army truck had shown up just in time. The sergeant saw a drunken soldier floating face down in the bay. He wouldn't have drowned— drunks never do. The men threw him on the truck and hurried back to finish their beer before their trucks came along. Montez didn't know why the military was doing this, picking them up in trucks; but he knew that it was a bad sign. He had been in the service long enough to know they would make you hurry, then they would make you wait. Who "they" were didn't matter. It was the Government and they were GIs—the lowest form of critter on earth.

A couple of minutes later, two trucks careened to a stop in the sand, loudspeakers blaring. The airmen jumped into one truck and a couple sailors into the other. As they sped to their barracks, Montez knew instinctively this was a turning point in his life—for better or worse it remained to be seen.

The young men were excited and a little scared at the same time. America was at war! They found the airbase in an uproar. Airmen rushed everywhere. After changing into their fatigues, they jumped onto a truck and were shuttled to their aircraft.

Montez asked, while holding tightly to the truck's wooden rails, "Ed, what you think about being at war and all that stuff?"

"Don't know what to think. But hell, Monty, they won't be shooting at us mechanics."

Ed added, "Maybe they'll land commandos to blow up the planes or even the barracks."

Montez, still nursing a hangover, replied, "I hope you're right. Maybe they'll land commandos to blow up the planes or some stuff like that." Placing his hand on his friend's shoulder, "Ed, don't you worry none—I'll take care of you. You'll be as safe as if you were in those Tennessee hills drinking moonshine."

"Boy, if there's commandos sent, they'll be after you ugly people so watch yore step."

As the truck dropped off crew members at their aircraft, Montez saw a changed flight line: armed guards; armament specialists carrying wooden boxes of bomb fuzzes; trucks scurrying to each B-29 with flack mats, flack suits, metal aircrew helmets and other equipment; ground crew personnel crawling over uncowled engines like ants.

"Are you airmen assigned to this plane?" asked a burly guard as Montez and Edwards jumped off the truck and walked to their plane.

After assuring the guard, Edwards commented to Montez, "He thinks we're saboteurs with hangovers."

Montez shot a backward look at the guard. "I think we better be careful with those idiots.

They have guns."

They joined their crew, busy working on the huge R-3350 engine for the trip. Montez scrambled up on top of the wing, shielding his eyes with his already oily hand. He stood frozen taking in a spectacle of orderly confusion as far as he could see. What astounded him most was his feeling that a huge hand was keeping things in order. Monster fuel trucks were rolling down the flight line, barely missing trucks and jeeps, and ponderously stopping at each aircraft to fill the large rubber-like tanks in each bomber's wings. He knew that they had trained for this for years but didn't think it would work so efficiently.

His bemusement was abruptly broken by an exasperated crew chief. "Montez, what the hell are you doing? Go help Smitty get that gear in the rear hatch."

The aircrew was checking the B-29, inside and out. Montez could feel their excitement and apprehension. He wished he were one of them, a waist gunner, and were going with them. He realized they could be killed, but not really…not yet.

Their bomber left before dawn the next day, but they were not told where. Ordered to pack everything they had, they rushed back to the barracks and then were told to wait in readiness.

Two days passed and they were still waiting. The news from Korea was not good. The North Koreans were pushing the United Nations forces down the Korean peninsula. The bad news dribbling in made the ground crew even more anxious to join their aircraft. The airmen could not go off the base, and the delay began to get on their nerves.

They were reduced to listening to Airmen Jones' and Garcia's, "hurry up and wait" routine. Garcia, in a deep voice, boomed, "I want you ready at a moment's notice. Your country expects you boys in Air Force blues to bomb them back to the Stone Age!"

Jonesy, in falsetto, "I'm ready, sir...." He was interrupted by a sergeant who ordered them to report to the flight line with all of their gear.

The crew quickly packed and shoved their gear into the ubiquitous 6X6 truck, and drove to the flight line where they boarded a waiting C-54 transport, along with what Montez thought were VIPs. Well, they must be important he thought. They were at least forty years old, and he didn't know anyone that old who wasn't a high-ranking officer or civilian.

The flight was not too long; but the closer they came to their destination—Okinawa, the more their apprehension rose. Montez had read the island's history, including what happened during World War II—one of the bloodiest campaigns in the Pacific with more than 90 percent of the island's buildings destroyed. But that didn't tell him much about the present. He recalled that the Okinawans were a mixture of Chinese and Japanese—Japan finally taking control from China early in the seventeenth century. Just as the sun was setting, he spotted the island. It must be Okinawa. It was the largest island he had seen during the transport's slow descent. When deplaned, he groaned in disappointment. The island wasn't as lush and resplendent as Guam; but, conversely, it was not as hot and humid. Gear in hand, he walked to the waiting truck thinking this was going to be all right—lower humidity and less heat. Kadena Air Force Base looked like Andersen Air Force Base in Guam, but busier—it definitely would be a welcome change. He didn't know about the mosquitoes.

Chapter 2

Okinawa

As the crew was bussed directly from the C-54 transport to the mess hall, eager eyes looked out bug-spattered bus windows, taking in a fast-moving panorama of airmen crawling all over B-29 bombers, revving engines and stacks of bombs of various sizes at every hardstand.

The excitement level of the men did not subside until they arrived at the biggest mess hall Montez had ever seen. Over two hundred, twenty-foot-long tables full of airmen and a scattering of soldiers, sailors and Marines filled the huge noisy hall. And blessed be the Almighty, hordes of serving girls! There were no girls in Guam, at least not for regular guys. The GIs from Guam and other locations had seen few women and couldn't take their hungry eyes off the young waitresses. Some of the girls were pretty, but most were stubby and plain, and completely preoccupied with the demands of their jobs. The air buzzed with excitement—the clanking of pans and utensils, the smell of food, sweaty bodies and testosterone.

It was bound to happen with all of these horny GIs and all those girls. A female shriek sounded in the mess hall, benches screeched and men talked in loud tones. Montez saw the Air Police escort out two GIs. Gesturing wildly with their arms, the GIs looked like they were proclaiming their innocence, but the Air Police stoically marched them out. Montez saw two Okinawan girls, one rubbing her behind, telling a sergeant what they did to them. You don't fool around with girls working at the air base, he thought.

The airman eating off a heaping metal tray beamed to Montez, "Man, they must have a jillion girls in this place. I've never seen so many girls. And some are pretty."

"I can hardly wait to go to town and see what's happening," replied Montez, as he waved a large coffee cup to a sweet-looking waitress carrying a gallon-size metal pitcher of coffee. He really didn't want coffee, just wanted to be next to a girl and say a few words to her.

The ground crew didn't get off the base for nearly a month. They worked on their aircraft every night under large bright lights. Montez couldn't believe how proficient they became changing those huge engines practically overnight while simultaneously working on other priorities. Their plane was constantly on bombing runs to North Korea and needed attention on a daily basis. There were not enough bombers to do the job, but the crew knew more planes were on the way from the States. The days and nights became jumbled in Montez's mind — there was just a passage of time.

One night, Montez looked wearily at Edwards, "You know, I'll never forget these nights as long as I live, especially that song, 'Come On-A My House,' by Rosemary Clooney. It's on the radio every hour."

"The only thing I'll remember is learning to sleep with my eyes open," grumbled Edwards as he tried to manhandle an engine supercharger cover in place.

Finally, relief for the crew and the rest of the Far East Air Forces in Japan and Okinawa came with loaned B-29 groups from the U.S. Air Force's Strategic Air Command stationed in the United States.

Two days later, Edwards and Montez took a break in the shade under the wing. "Can you believe it?" Edwards commented, "I heard that they sent the new B-29 groups from the States to Japan. Here we are in this goddamned place with no 'wimmen,' no nothing."

"Quit your bitching, Ed. With these new groups, we can get off this frigging base and find those wild women."

"Yeah, poontang and beer are waiting for this ol' boy," sighed Edwards.

"You damned hillbilly…you wouldn't know

what to do with those little gals, even with instructions."

Finally, the crew got leave. Montez and Edwards had talked incessantly about what they would do and how many girls they would bed. They ended up calmly touring as many villages as they could in a rented pedicab—a bicycle pulling a platform on wheels with wooden bench seats—with sufficient beer to keep them content.

The villages were mostly small—one hundred people or so. Montez couldn't believe how poor the people were.

"Do you think they have always lived this poor? The Guamanians lived much better than this."

"Well," replied Edwards, "I've seen the old mamasans go through our trash and use just about everything they find."

"Now I know why there are so many young working girls," Montez added. "I saw the same thing along the Mexican border."

"I'm going to avail myself of some of those 'working girls,' as you call 'em," leered Edwards, "and soon."

Surveying the reconstruction of Naha, the capital of Okinawa, Montez noticed that their young pedicab driver, while trying to appear unconcerned, was listening to everything they said. He's as interested in us as we are in them, thought Montez.

"We destroyed the towns he just took us to.

Strange how history works—who would we be bombing after this war is over?"

Edwards finally remarked after, for him, a long period of silence, "I guess we're doing the same thing in North Korea right now…probably not cities, though."

"This isn't the first time and sure as hell won't be the last. I just hope no one decides to make the bombs nuclear." With a perceptible movement of his body as if to shake the somber thoughts away, Montez added, "What the hell are we talking about? Let's get drunk before we get any older…but first let's find some girls!"

There were as many girls as they wanted. Entering a large village restaurant-bar, a pudgy girl in an olive-green cotton skirt and a garish orange top marched up to Edwards and asked, "Hey GI, two dolla one timo? Good time, ne?"

Edwards gaped at her. "No way little gal."

"What the hell do we do now?" Edwards asked an amused Montez.

Before Montez could answer, a girl grabbed his arm. "You buy me biro, ne? I give you good time."

It was Montez's turn to be speechless. Trying to be sophisticated, he put his arm around her shoulder and turned to Edwards. "I think we ought to at least buy these gals a drink."

They sat down at a rickety table covered in a checkered oilcloth and ordered beer. They felt pretty good about their accomplishment until an old army sergeant sitting at the next table grumbled, "You know, you new guys shot up prices of everything on this damn island when you got here. Pretty soon, tail will cost more than two dollars. And why in hell are you buying them beer. Pretty soon they will expect that, too!" Balancing on his small chair, Montez, with his newly acquired insouciant demeanor, said "Don't worry, Sarge, we're not buying them beer. I guess cokes are okay." The sergeant grunted, turned away with disgust and took a long swig of his Nippon beer, thinking the Air Force was recruiting little kids out of grammar school.

Montez and Edwards looked about themselves curiously. The brightly lit unpainted room was about twelve-feet wide and twenty-two-feet long, with four large and four small tables. Nearly every table was busy with drinking airmen and their female companions. Montez noted that most of the girls drank sodas. Several of the girls were sitting together near the entrance, giggling and making suggestive gestures to unattached airmen. He found the scene picturesque and wished he had a camera so he could send a picture to his brother back in God's country.

One of the chatting girls caught his attention; she was pretty, a slender figure, adorned by a loose western dress, high-heel shoes, and bright-red lipstick, showing even white teeth when she smiled. It was her sad-looking eyes above a tiny nose that belied her giggles and held his interest.

Montez must have stared at her too long; she forced a smile and walked over to his table.

"I've found mine," he whispered to Edwards, "and is she a doll."

"Hello, GI, my name is Lana. You buy me soda?"

"Sure. Please sit down. I'm Monty. This goofy GI is my friend, Ed."

Edwards was nonplussed for a moment and then regained what he considered his irresistible charm. "Why yore a pretty gal, Lana — too pretty for my diseased friend here. Not serious, mind you; just a social disease."

"You funny GI. I get you my friend. Ichiban girl, numbah one girl, make you velly hoppy."

Lana waved at her girl friend who was obviously waiting for the invitation. She was not as pretty as Lana, but Edwards was more than satisfied with the short compact girl with huge breasts.

"I tell you, boy," Edwards said, as he found a chair for her at the table, "I'm going to graze on those bazookas like a starving jack rabbit in a garden."

"I'm Betty. You tocusan GI, like velly high," she pointed to the ceiling, "You buy me soda, ne?"

"Anything you want, musume." Edwards heard that's Okinawan for "girl." "Anything yore little ol' heart desires."

Montez thought he heard the old army sergeant at the next table mutter, "Goddamn punk kids ruining everything."

The evening quickly passed with beer and talk, mostly between Montez and Edwards. Lana finally grabbed Montez' arm and said, "Maybe we go bed now. You stay with me all night, ne?"

Montez looked at a grinning Edwards and said nonchalantly, "Why sure, it's getting late."

Led by the girls, they went through a side door, out to an alley and into a wood house divided into four six-by-ten-foot rooms. Montez followed Lana down a dimly lit, narrow corridor and into the far corner room. Edwards and Betty went into the room next to them.

Lana turned the light on, and Montez saw a short table with a lamp and ashtray next to a clean bedroll. A small rack with nondescript clothes hugged the wall at the foot of the bedroll. She closed the door. He felt large, clumsy and nervous; so he busied himself studying pictures of Japanese movie stars on the wall until he came upon an old snapshot of an older couple and two children, one obviously Lana. She pulled him away from the picture, started to undress him until he stopped her.

"I can do that," he said unbuttoning his shirt, and then sat on the bed not knowing if he should continue.

"You bashful boy," she said rubbing his cheek like he was a cat. "Maybe you cherry boy?"

"I'm no cherry boy. I have many girls stateside."

She undid her dress and let it fall on the floor, "I think you first time boy." Montez stared at a small, perfectly formed body and couldn't move as she unhooked her bra. He caught sight of small breasts with large brown nipples before she turned out the light.

"Why did you turn the light off?" He wanted to look at her some more but didn't know how to insist. Her small hands undid his trousers, pulled him gently to the bedroll, and then he felt her lips search for his.

"Much nicer in dark, you feel bettah." The last thing he remembered thinking was how silky her skin felt.

Montez and Edwards, as well as their air and ground crew's visits to the villages were for short periods of time; but as the days slowly rolled on into weeks, they got into a tenuous routine at the village. Montez was now used to seeing whole villages full of whorehouses. It was normal to walk into a village and see the girls hanging around doorways selling their wares. Sometimes he felt that old empty feeling in the bottom of his stomach when he saw dirty little kids running around picking up cigarette butts thrown away by GIs. Memories of Mexican border towns he had visited rushed into his head and left as quickly.

"Christ, look at those kids! What do you think the locals think of us?" He asked Edwards one day while strolling through a small village.

"Hell, boy, I don't think of it. Neither should

you. We didn't create this mess…or those kids you worry about. Shit, there are poor people at home, so why get in an uproar over this?"

Montez shrugged his shoulders, "You're right, it's bad in a lot places, but still…hell, let's grab a beer before we head back."

There was also a routine on the flight line. Their plane, the "Pesky Fly," was now bombing bridges near the Yalu River and "accidently" hitting targets in China. At least that was the scuttlebutt among the crews. At any rate, lot of B-29's had been shot down or badly damaged. The Pesky Fly had finished its 60th mission, more than any other B-29 in this "police action" as the war was called. The ground crew was proud of their record, keeping the old warplane flying. Montez received a newspaper picture and a small written article from the Bakersfield Californian from his brother. It showed him and part of his crew pointing to the row of painted bombs on his plane's fuselage.

One morning Montez awoke and groggily staggered from his bunk. He looked at his watch — 4:00 a.m. — and then at his crumply sheets. The mosquito netting and the insecticide buzz-bomb didn't work. Every night before he went to sleep, he tucked in the mosquito netting under the mattress, then sprayed the inside of the bed and mosquito netting with insecticide — to no avail. The mosquitoes got in somehow; the only thing he was poisoning was himself. The sheets were red with his blood and blood-engorged mosquitoes he had crushed turning over in his sleep. God, he thought, how he hated mosquitoes.

By the time Montez got to the flight line an hour later, the revetments, housing their respective bombers, glowed under huge lights. Far away, he could hear the sound of heavy engines coughing awake as if they, too, wanted to sleep a little longer. When they reached their revetment, Montez jumped off the truck, along with the other ground and aircrews. He saw his crew chief, a large, muscular older man, already inspecting the aircraft. "Old" meant over 35, a Methuselah by the Montez's standards. Most airmen were trying to look 21 and legal for any bar or nightclub in the world.

Montez could never get used to the eerie sight: dozens of B-29 bombers, huge four-engine aircraft, each loaded with eight tons of bombs, and hundreds of men calmly preparing their planes and themselves to go into harm's way. The heavy metallic creatures groaned into formation for takeoff, their brakes screeching as each turned from its revetment to its place in line. Watching the line of bombers, Montez could see the shiny skin of the aircraft engine's nacelles reflecting the red flames thrusting into the darkness of the early morning. The noise from the revving engines was mind numbing, yet the ground crew had to check for safety problems. Finally, it was over. The bombers were on their way. With luck, this would be a "milk run," an easy mission, as the planes carried a heavy bomb load and a light gas load. They were not going to the Chinese border this time.

Once the bombers were gone, the absence of the aircraft's roar affected Montez more than the noise and excitement of the takeoff. A feeling of loss came over him as the bright lights were turned off. A pinkish tinge signaled another hot day as the sun peeked over the horizon and the silence of the jungle again engulfed them.

The ground crew was free for the day. Every small group of friends planned something. Montez assumed Edwards was preparing a scenario in which he would find some beer, a fight and some bad women. Not that Edwards liked to fight—he was a lover. Montez, on the other hand, was still in training to be a great lover.

"Monty, you have to listen to me when it comes to women. Don't let them know you're after them or they'll be after your ass." Edwards was his mentor, and he never let Montez forget it until he found that Edwards didn't know any more than he did.

Montez and his friend worked out a system to get away from the rest of the guys. They liked to go off by themselves, away from the clamorous crowd, and just talk about mankind, good and bad. Both of them said they just wanted to get away from the crowd. It was more than that, Montez suspected, but he couldn't put it into words. He was not alienated from his Mexican-American friends. They got along fairly well. But sometimes he still felt he didn't belong. Montez wasn't part of the group. He wasn't part of any group. They were onstage, and Montez was part of the audience. Growing up in the San Joaquin Valley as a poor Mexican-American and a loner had been a misery. He was beat up by the "Okies" when they could catch him, and shunned as an oddball by his fellow Mexican-Americans. His only real friend was his younger brother, but he had his own problems. Montez felt he was walking a thin line: on one side his extended family and the other, the great Anglo majority. He had acquaintances on both sides and felt each pulling him.

His only refuge was an escape to the library and books. He lived in the library when not working at whatever job he could drum up. Books saved him and his soul from perdition, he believed. He read voraciously, insatiably, savoring every moment like it was his last, and felt as if he lost a loved one after he finished a delicious novel. Suddenly he was no longer the wandering Odysseus, Beowulf with his magnificent boar-helmet, Aeneas, son of Venus, or Walter finding the beautiful black rose in ancient Cathay. But yet, he knew they would always be there, to be read and re-read for the rest of his life.

Edwards apparently felt the same way with his peers. He got along with his good-ol'-boy friends, talked their talk, but underneath he was not part of the group.

As he put it, "I just get tired of talking about boozing, hunting, and football. Now talking 'bout wimen… that's different."

Airman 2nd Class Ulysses Virgil Edwards always had a quick smile, but he aggravated Montez because he always got the best-looking girls. They were drawn to his looks: handsome — with a boyish innocence that attracted the opposite sex. Other GIs didn't understand his way with women and sometimes tried to change his looks the hard way. He also joined the service to find himself and high adventure. His family was dirt poor, and he was always a little hungry — probably filling a growing six-foot four-inch frame by the time he was fourteen. He was now six-foot six-inches tall and he worried about getting taller.

Being his friend, thought Montez, was not always easy. He remembered their first meeting at the library in Guam. Edwards was putting the make on some officer's daughter and didn't see the Captain, her father, coming up behind him.

Without thinking, Montez boomed out with authority, "Edwards, you're wanted at the Operations Room immediately."

Edwards turned to him, saw her father out of the corner of his eye, and said, "Well, ah have to be off. Nice talking to you."

With a few fast strides of his long legs, he was at Montez's side. "Boy, ah owe you one. Ah hear that bastard's mean as a constipated bull."

Montez wondered why he got involved with

a relative stranger. Every time he did something like that, and he did it often, he got in some kind of trouble. Like that time in Delano when that big Cholo was beating up a farmworker, and he told him to leave him alone. The little guy ran off and Montez got his ass whipped for his trouble.

"I was going to the library...." Montez began.

"Yeah, me too, until I saw that pretty little ol' thing and decided to reconnoiter," Edwards broke in.

This started a string of events that Montez felt verified his contention about trouble. He and Edwards were in some kind of hot water from that day on.

They were a strange pair, always together, yet from completely different backgrounds: Edwards, a relaxed, soft-spoken Southerner, and Montez a reserved, introspective Mexican-American from Central California.

While having a few beers at the Airman's Club a few weeks later, Edwards told Montez, "You know my good ol' country friends don't understand why I don't go to the village with them."

"Hell, my friends say the same thing," replied Montez and added mischievously. "They can't understand why I hang out with an ugly redneck."

"You just listen to this ol' redneck and I'm going to teach you just 'bout everything you'll ever need."

"Christ," replied Montez, trying not to laugh. "You can't even speak like a decent everyday American. Learn to pronounce some simple words so that civilized society can understand you."

Edwards liked to talk like an uneducated hillbilly; and although he only had a high school education, he read every book he got his hands on. Montez felt that was why he and Edwards, so dissimilar in temperament and background, got along so well. Unfortunately, Montez had only finished the eleventh grade and Edwards like to lord it over him. Edwards was "edicated" and had a piece of paper showing he graduated from high school.

"Ed, my pappy told me, 'para tonto no se estudia' which means, one needn't study to be a fool." Montez added. "You reached your goal."

"Why that there foreign gibberish is not real American. Ah don't cotton to fools except for you."

Montez, however, was taking courses from the U.S. Armed Forces Institute and would soon get his high school diploma. He also finished some college level courses and warned Edwards, "I'm leaving you behind, my boy; so you better take some courses with me."

In a serious tone of voice, Edwards said, "One ol' boy that really doesn't understand...or like it, is our assistant crew chief Sergeant Easley. He thinks you're... well, like a foreigner."

"Hell, if that's all, I'm in like Flynn. I've been called just about everything from wetback to wop."

In the end, they both came to the same conclusion—if their friends didn't like it, they could shove it.

Pronunciation of certain words became a running joke between them. Both had picked up much of their vocabulary from reading books by Homer, Milton and Tennyson. They didn't realize that much of their vocabulary was out of common use. The dictionary was their bible, and they memorized the meaning of words but often didn't know quite how to pronounce them. Their family and friends, even their teachers, didn't use those words so they never heard them used.

"Ed, you're supposed to say procurement, pronounced cure, not cur, like a dog."

"How do you know? You can't even pronounce dawg, you illiterate wetback!"

One morning, Montez found Edwards reading a pocketbook dictionary while sitting on one of a long line of commodes. Ten feet across from him was a corresponding line of commodes with three young housekeeping girls sitting on toilets smiling at them. Montez had gotten used to having the cleaning girls use the pots while he was there. Nevertheless, he didn't like it so he usually made sure the girls were gone before he used the latrine.

He took a stool next to Edwards, and after

some choice words on his friend's uncouth practices, said, "I can't believe that anyone would read the dictionary while taking a crap," Montez added, "No wonder you can't speak English."

Edwards sat up imperiously on his throne and haughtily replied, "Listen boy, I am the most educated soul in this man's Air Force. Ah just have no one to have an intellectual conversation with, someone who understands my meanings—you ain't no help either."

One day Montez asked, "Ed, why did you join the Air Force? Did they run you off the old homestead?"

"Well, I did kind of run off from home, so to speak, but I wanted to travel mostly."

"I'll be damned. I really ran away from home. I couldn't get along with the folks, but, also, I wanted to see the world."

Propinquity. They were in the same ground crew; their eclectic discussions on religion, philosophy, and growing up as outsiders in their hometowns solidified their friendship. Montez and Edwards conspired to marry each other's younger sister, consequently cementing kin, and then getting into some business—preferably a brothel, which Edwards would manage while Montez played the piano and hired the help.

"How come you get to hire the help?" Edwards questioned. "I'm the manager; I should do the hiring."

"I'm a better judge of women and don't you

forget it," opined Montez. "Remember how you always trust the musumes and get taken every time? Besides I can't play the piano all the time."

The major impediment to this business arrangement was Edwards' sister. She was ugly as sin and looked to be nearly as tall as Edwards in a picture, but Montez didn't say a word because it would probably hurt Edwards' feelings. Ed was very sentimental.

So, when they left the base, they looked for women and adventures far from the ordinary as possible, which also meant getting as far away as possible from the southern part of the island where most of the population lived and GIs frequented. During their journeys throughout the mountains and jungles of the northern section of the island, they found caves, ancient weed-covered tombs, and parts of rotted, scarred military equipment.

One day, Montez found what looked like the remnants of an old Japanese army belt in the soft sand-like earth. "I bet whoever wore this is with his ancestors. Hey, this looks like army leggings." He held up mildewed scraps of brown cloth. "I saw pictures of Japanese soldiers wearing these."

"Yep, looks like Japanese soldiers lived here."

Once Edwards found a rusted hand grenade and a long thin Japanese bayonet under a bush. Before he could pick it up, Montez yelled, "Don't touch that! It could blow your ass off."

Edwards yanked his hand back as if burned. "God damn, boy," Edwards bellowed, "You scared the piss out of me!"

"OK, next time I'll let you blow up…when I'm far away." Montez plodded off into the bush.

One day, in one of their deeper forays into the caves, Edwards found some old, well-preserved pottery and cooking utensils half buried in the soft earth. They also unearthed animal bones — hopefully they were animal bones — and imagined a family cooking their dinner in this cave hundreds of years ago.

"See these two little bowls?" Montez held up some pieces of pottery. "They were used by two kids and the larger bowls by the parents."

"Hell, how do you know that? That looks more like the remains of a shattered vase. Next you'll be telling me their names."

"The kid's names are Akira and little Keiko with a deformed leg…."

"Okay, goddamn it," Edwards broke in feigning disgust.

They were going to take what looked like utensils: wooden sticks with carved markings and large, chipped wooden spoons. But they decided to leave them.

"These things have been here for years. Let's not disturb the ghosts." Montez whispered.

Edwards dropped the spoon he was inspecting, as if it had bit his hand. "Damn, boy! This here hole is spooky 'nough without you talking 'bout ghosts. You going Asiatic on me or what?"

Later, Montez tried to bury something in the dirt, but Edwards caught him. "What the hell you doing there, boy?"

"I'm leaving some script." Montez dug in his khakis for more money. "Let some one from a future war, maybe in 2051, find it. They'll say some American soldier dropped it in 1951."

"Monty, you're crazy as hell!"

They left the cave a few minutes later. With a last look at the dark interior, Montez said, half-joking, "I think we were a little possessed in there. I felt as if someone was in there with us. Not a demon or a devil, just a waiting spirit."

Edwards was beside himself. "Listen, boy, I know you're one of them atheists, funning things you don't know 'bout. I know there's fairy folk, and old Beelzebub is ready to get you."

Montez decided to leave it alone. Edwards was as rational a person as he'd ever met, but when it came to the supernatural, the "little people" seemed to take control. At least Edwards seemed earnest when he talked about it. He was a large part Irish—that probably explained it.

Still, unable to help himself, Montez added one final though for Edwards' edification, "You know, you may be right. I didn't say anything because I don't believe in ghosts. But I saw an apparition, a wraith-like specter, looking at us from the part of the cave we didn't go into."

"Goddamn! There you go again. Now you

tell me the truth. Did you really see something?"

Montez just smiled and shook his head, as if it he didn't want to talk about it. Ribbing Edwards was one thing, but Montez did feel strange in the cave, particularly when he impulsively left the money. He felt he had become part of history. For moment, he even imagined he was the person finding the money one hundred years later.

That evening, they went to a new restaurant, the New Ginza, and drank Nippon beer with a couple of local girls. It was in an open area, with just enough trees to make it interesting, not too far from the airbase, good Japanese music and quiet. It was compatible with their temperament.

Edwards continued pumping him for more information on the cave. "Com'on Monty, was that a goblin you saw in the cave? I can tell you stories of banshees in the hills where I grew up."

"Christ's sake, Ed, forget about those things! Next you'll be telling me about how you chased the little people."

"What I don't understand is that you said your folks are Catholic, yet you're a damned atheist."

"I'm a cultural Catholic with all the problems that brings. And I'm one of those lazy atheists — an agnostic."

With each additional beer, they delved into the mysteries of life, as far as very young men understood it, and tried to figure out why they were such misfits. It wasn't just in the military, they decided.

Montez thought about the problems he had at home. "You know in civilian life I felt like I was a backward trout spawning downstream. All my life I've been trying to be like everyone else — to fit in with the boys. It didn't work, so I went the other way. I sat in the back row in school hoping no one would notice me, lived a heroic life in books, and hoped no one would notice me until I became famous and rich."

"Hot damn! I did the same thing," exclaimed Edwards. "The only difference was I was smart and got close to the gals."

"You weren't smart, just horny."

They figured they'd learn where they belonged… in time. They had nearly two years on this island to learn about fitting round pegs into square holes. It wouldn't be sporting to put a round peg in a round hole — at least, not for them.

Later, they cuddled up to their girlfriends in their little rooms. Through the thin wooden wall, Montez heard Edwards' final inspiration. "You know, I'm doing just fine for a country boy. You're doing OK for a double ugly. We're keeping these here musumes happy. And that's more than most can say."

"Go to sleep, ridge runner. We got that B-29 waiting for us tomorrow… and we may be stuck on base for a long time."

Chapter 3

The Village

The closest town to the U.S. Airbase was actually two small villages separated by a hill. Usually the U.S. servicemen separated their visit to each village by race: Blacks in one village and everyone else in the other. No one knew how this started or when, but it was a normal event; if one went to the wrong village, you automatically kept walking over the hill to where you "belonged." Although the President had stopped segregation in the Armed Forces in 1946, the servicemen still segregated themselves. The villages were small with the indigenous people living there for the primary purpose of serving the GIs. When the villages started or became inhabited by the Okinawans for that purpose, no one knew, nor did anyone care.

Airmen 2nd Class Montez and Edwards finally got off the base after three days and nights of working nearly nonstop on their aircraft. The sky was a bright light blue with a sprinkling of fluffy white clouds, making them feel so elated that they decided to splurge on a four-seat pedicab. Montez noted the driver's skinny muscular legs pumped slowly, then faster as the cab picked up speed once on the paved road.

"I bet we couldn't keep up pedaling a bike like these guys do," Montez said. "They may be small, but they sure are hardy."

"Well, maybe you couldn't, but I used to race my bicycle straight up the Great Smoky Mountains in East Tennessee," Edwards added. "No one could keep up with me." Once they got onto the dirt road leading to the village, it got interesting.

"Yeah, I know," Montez replied. "And you composed the Tennessee Waltz on the way up."

Once on the dirt road leading to the village, they saw the villagers working in their rolled-up brown trousers in the rice paddies or small farms: variegated green and yellow crops, surrounded by a darker verdure of hedged bushes intertwined with brown-green vines.

Edwards, sniffing the air like a blood hound, said, "This island is older than man and twice as smelly."

The odor of manure, rotting vegetation, new foliage and fried tofu layered the valley and the surrounding jungle, all the way to the hills in the background. Giggling teenagers in bright-colored dresses, with sturdy brown legs clopped their way on wooden sandals. "I'd like to talk to some of those fillies," Edwards said with a leer,

"But looks like they have a mamasan for an escort."

"Ed, look, that old mamasan has an ammo box on her head…it must weigh over a hundred pounds."

"Yeah, I heard that these old women can carry that weight on their heads for miles."

They stared at the fifty-plus-year-old woman, her back straight as an arrow, with only a braided straw padding on her head, as she balanced a large wooden ammunition box full of food and other items. They nodded their heads in admiration as they continued on their way, bouncing and swaying over dusty potholes.

They were nearing the village. Greenery gave way to open ground and weeds. Everything was brown, including a slatted wood house with a stoop in front surrounded by packed earth. The upper part of the house had brightly painted Japanese writing and a colorful picture of a hamburger and an old Coke sign. They got closer to the village and its slatted wood structures. Everything was brown here, including the hut with a stoop or porch in front and the packed earth. A sign above the restaurant, house of assignation and bar, labeled "The New Ginza" in garish red letters, was followed by a smaller sign, "G.I. welcome. No fight. No drunk." The inside was plain, functional and clean—two bare wood tables with tattered, faded yellow menus, wood bench seats, and thin wood walls decorated with old

Japanese calendars picturing beautiful girls, and the ubiquitous beer ads. Montez knew the New Ginza wasn't much, but it was their place. They spent many a night and day, drinking beer, discussing the merits of women in general, and their current female companions, in particular. Today, a couple of lazy hours drinking beer was enough—they didn't know what to do next.

Ennui…that's the problem, Montez said.

"What the hell you mumbling about, boy?"

"We're bored," Montez added, "We got to do something different. In fact, I have studying to do. Let's go back to the base."

It wasn't like there was no place else to go at the airbase since the NCO Club catered to military personnel. The L-shaped club had tables of various sizes, red or white tablecloths usually soaked with beer spilled from large pitchers, and ashtrays overflowing with wet ashes and cigarette butts. Although full of loud, boisterous men, the NCO Club still managed to look Spartan and bleak—a place one went for a purpose—to get soused, and for some to forget for a short while that they were away from home. Some got on each other's nerves and about once a month, a night there ended in a donnybrook.

One evening, Montez and Edwards decided to go to the Club instead of the village, and got caught in an altercation. Montez didn't know how it started, but since it was on the other side of the large room and a common occurrence, they didn't pay much attention. They overheard the men on the next table talking about home, how great their mother cooked, and how they could hardly wait to get back to civilization.

"Ed, do you believe that stuff about how everybody has such a great family and home?"

"Well, I can tell you that most of the old boys I know sure as hell don't have much waiting for them at home."

As Montez and Edwards continued their conversation, the brawl spread in to their direction so they crawled under the table with their pitcher of beer to enjoy the free-for-all.

Montez exclaimed, "I don't think those drunken bastards can see us behind the table-cloth."

They were innocently, as they later put it, looking at the drunken brawl from under the table, enjoying their beer, and minding their own business, and cheering when soldiers and airmen went skidding past them on their back on the beer soaked hardwood floor.

Edwards gulped his beer, "Hot damn boy, I think that big sum bitch saw us and doesn't look happy."

A huge, irate Marine sergeant spotted them, picked up their small round table, and hit them over the head with the tabletop. To indicate their displeasure, the Marine and his buddies threw the dazed airmen out of the window. Fortunately, the window glass was open and they went through the screen rolling down a rock-strewn hill.

Montez nursed his swimming head saying, "Marines have never been known to have a sense of humor. I'm glad I didn't join those fools."

Edwards glumly added, "I can't understand why those dumb jarheads can't see that I'm a lover, not a fighter." Edwards glumly added, gingerly touching his head, "I kicked the one trying to hold my leg in the head before he could get a good hold. I think he bit my leg."

"Come on, ridge-runner, let's go get some clean duds and go to Mamasan's for some beer. First, I need some tape to pull this cut on my head together or I'll get blood all over me again."

"I don't know, Monty. I got a headache and got blood all over me. I gotta take a shower and make sure that Jireen didn't infect my leg — they don't brush their teeth, you know. I might even get rabies."

"Okay, Ed, tomorrow is another day, so let's start early."

Whenever they stopped at the New Ginza for a cold beer, Mamasan would greet them with a huge grin and, "Hello GI — two birus, ne?" She never greeted them by name, although they had known each other for over one year, and they always called her Mamasan. They liked going to the village early in the day, when there were few GIs around. They could relax before the loud music started in earnest. On the days when their plane would leave in the early morning, they could hit the village when it was empty. Consequently, this was a place of quiet and repose, and they agreed that Karma had placed them in this spot for a purpose: to drink and philosophize about life, thereby helping humanity. How they could do that would be revealed by a superior force.

During their countless discussions, Edwards came to the conclusion that Montez needed to have his head examined; he couldn't understand why Montez distrusted Gringos, even after Montez explained how they had treated him because he was of Mexican descent.

"You saw those signs stating 'No Mexicans or dogs allowed' on the windows of some of those joints in Wichita Falls, Texas."

"Well, hell boy, just don't admit to being one — you can be whoever you want to be."

"I'll never do that. I like the way we are and look. Wait till you see some of those Mexican-American girls. Trouble is they won't give you a break."

Edwards only knew of Negroes and American Indians, and he was proud that his grand mammy had been a full-blooded Cherokee.

"There are other minorities besides Negroes and Indians," Montez explained. "Ever heard of Oriental people; and, to make your little brain hurt even more, one can be of Mexican descent and be a Jew, European, Black or Indian, with all variations and mixtures. Like being an American, it's not a race, but a nationality."

"Well, am I one of those damned Gringos?" asked Edwards. "I didn't do anything. Do you trust me?"

Putting his arm around Edwards' shoulders, Montez answered, "Ed, you're so dumb, you can't tree a possum. Therefore, I trust you. Besides, you have some good Injun blood in you, so we're blood brothers."

Edwards still couldn't figure out Montez's problem. "Hell, you look like me and act like me, so why not be like me and stay out of trouble."

"Are you crazy? The last thing I want is to be like you and act like you. Then I would have to hate people that don't look or act like me."

"Boy, you are getting me mighty confused."

They would argue the situation for hours, happily imbibing beer and thanking the first brew master of the world. One of the many things discussed was what they were really going to do after they were discharged. Both of them joked that if the officers had college degrees, then they too could breeze through college.

"Do you really think we could make it through college?" asked Montez. "I want to do that more than anything else. Guess I always have."

"Hey, you're the thinker. Everybody believes you're smart except you."

"All right, we'll both go to college when we get out."

Because Edwards didn't want to return to Tennessee, after some spirited discussion, they agreed to go to UCLA and then become million-aires.

"Ed, what are you going to major in?"

"Guess I'll get a degree in business and find where that dirty old money is hiding. What about you?"

Montez rested his chin on his hands, pondered for a while. "Law. I'm going to be a damned lawyer. They always have a job picking up money the rich…and the poor let slip out of their grasp."

"Well, this old boy is not going to hire you or any other damned shyster."

Montez grinned, "Just you wait. You'll need a smooth solicitor like me some day, then…gotcha."

At times trouble erupted in their little refuge. Fights broke out at the restaurant. Drunk GIs tore up the place. However, after the Air Police took the rowdies away, everything would calm down again. Edwards and Montez could again discuss the important things in life, for young men, and solve worldly problems until they got tired and went to their small rooms with their current girl friend to make love, kill mosquitoes and sleep. Before he went to sleep, Montez listened to the sounds of the Japanese stringed instrument. The samisen created an eerie and poignant lament flowing through the hills and valleys of the sleeping island. He felt lonely and far from home; he was fixed in time, inconsequential and powerless.

After a breakfast of beer and soba, the delicious noodle soup bought from the street merchant's pushcart, Montez and Edwards had to decide whether they should go back to the base and clean up, or head out to the seashore with their girlfriends to scuba dive and inspect the old wrecks sunk off the island during World War II.

They ended up on a part of the island that Okinawan friends told Montez about. Best of all, there were no GIs around. The warm water was a clear turquoise-blue or green hue, depending on the depth, underwater foliage and coral. The hot sand was full of small cockleshells, some sharp enough to cut your bare feet if you weren't careful. The young airmen always managed to find some soft sand with plenty of trees for shade, where they made love with their girlfriends.

Wading in the white coral-rimmed lagoon, Edwards, with his hands on his hips surveyed his domain and sighed, "Here we are, old top. Where else could you have the beverage of your choice, women at your whim and beauty at every turn?" Edwards liked to wax poetic at times. "My noble Irish ancestors gave the world beautiful verse and rhyme."

"Ed, you're descended from some hillbillies that lived in the Tennessee mountains. You wouldn't know a verse from a curse."

"Well, at least we don't sacrifice virgins on bloody altars."

"I heard that there are no virgins in Tennessee to sacrifice."

Finally lulled by the lapping sound of the lagoon, they slept in the shade of the trees. Later, they decided to explore the beach and go swimming in the buff. The girls didn't want to, but Edwards convinced them that the part of their skin covered by their swimsuit needed the sun. They didn't believe it, but it was a good excuse to swim naked and feel the sun.

Like all things, it had to come to an end, and they headed back to the airbase and reality.

Of course, reality was in the eyes of the beholder thought Montez. The airbase was a microcosm of the United States: Hollywood movies; plenty of food; English spoken everywhere, even by the natives working at the base; and an implicit belief that Americans were the best of all the conquering nations in the world. Did the Romans or British feel the same way? They were too cocky and too well fed; but right now, they were at the top of the food chain and Montez felt that they might as well enjoy it while they could.

Yet in the village, he felt somewhat uneasy when he talked to the local men whom he had befriended. They knew that he was of Mexican descent and told him things they would not tell other GIs. They felt Montez would understand their plight—a conquered nation full of swaggering soldiers, buying their women and destroying their island.

Montez agreed with them, in part, and told them that it had happened to all nations, when it was their time, throughout history. They would grumble assent and suck air through their teeth showing displeasure or agreement—Montez was never sure. The Okinawans were interested in Montez and how he was accepted in the States. They were more aware of what was happening in the world than Montez had imagined.

One of them once asked, "Montez-san, white people treat Mexico boy OK?"

"Some do, some don't. Some are no good, ba-catare, a fool like Edwards-san." Everybody knew Edwards was bacatare.

"But, if you study and work hard, the States is the place to be."

"Ah so, wakarimas, I understand."

Looking at the men's calloused hands and sunburned faces, Montez knew they would work hard and make something of themselves in the States.

Many of his Okinawan friends had relatives living in Latin America, and they were doing very well there. Mr. Ishizumi usually asked the questions for the rest of the men. He even knew some Spanish, which he practiced with "Mexico boy" as Montez was called. He didn't like being called that but didn't know how to stop it. Montez knew it was meant as a compliment because it separated him from the others. Mr. Ishizumi told him that his brother, a potter by trade, went to Peru in 1940 and had a small factory producing fine pottery.

"I go to America. Buy small land and buy more... soon get rich for family." He said this mixing English and Spanish to show he was an educated man.

Montez was also learning a lot from these conversations. They were not as complacent as he thought regarding the thousands of GIs on their island, especially the young men. Montez didn't get along as well with the young men; however, they treated him well enough. Although many of them had jobs because of the American presence, they also knew they were dismissed with "just some gooks."

"Hey Monty. What are you doing? Looks like you were in a trance."

"You are bacatare, Ed. Let's get these gals home."

Back at the airbase, Montez and Edwards were already talking about what they were going to do the next time they went to the village. They laughed at the remembrance of the spiffy Air Police at the base gate staring, with obvious disgust, at their disheveled uniforms and bloodshot eyes.

"You know, I kind of wish I had some of those nasty crabs we pick up occasionally," Edwards drawled. "I would have flipped a few to those APs and have them scratch their asses off for awhile."

A passing sergeant alerted them of tomorrow's mission and they reluctantly returned to reality.

Chapter 4

Typhoon

Montez lay on his bunk listening to the staccato wail of wind and rain. He found it oddly comforting that he liked this rain, monsoon or not. He had grown up in California's San Joaquin Valley wishing for rain to moisten the parched earth. Although the valley was full of trees and crops, most of the water came not from the sky but from aqueducts. He missed, however, the wide-open land leading to the far-off hazy mountains surrounding the valley.

Montez hoped that the powers in charge of typhoons knew what they were doing and were on the job. There was always some military specialist who took care of contingencies. Maybe there was a typhoon Military Occupational Specialty (MOS). The power-that-be, with a high clout MOS, ordered the bombers, jet fighters and other aircraft to be flown out of the storm's way. Montez and Edwards had worked two days straight getting their aircraft airworthy and packed with gear before the storm hit. The ground crew gave a collective sigh of relief when their plane finally lifted off to safety.

"What's the name of that '29 that flipped over like a pancake when the winds came? The one that was having its three engines changed and couldn't make it?"

"Don't know," replied Edwards as he eased out of his bunk. "But I know that the air and ground crews are going to be parceled out to other crews."

Breaking up his ground crew was the last thing Montez wanted. He could think of one person he could do without—Staff Sergeant Easley, assistant crew chief on his aircraft. Christ, what a piece of work he was. His reverie was interrupted by Edwards, who, as usual, was spouting off some hare-brained idea that usually got them into trouble.

"Here we are, newly promoted sergeants and nothing to do. Ya know we ought to make some of that snake sake they sell at the village. I saw them do it."

Edwards was talking and exercising—a forbidden action in his lengthy list of destructive acts that humans perform. His lanky frame was going in different directions at the same time. With a grimace, he stopped, grabbed his knobby knees and panted as if he had run four miles.

"Ed, you look like a skinny scarecrow on stilts ready to fall on your bony ass! You know we don't like that stuff. Anyway you don't know how to brew sake."

Edwards forgot about the sake and started on a long story regarding hurricanes. "Why hell, boy, I was in a real one in South Carolina a few years back. Now that was trouble—it lifted whole buildings and dropped them miles away with nary a scratch."

Flinging the mosquito netting on top of the bed frame, Montez replied, "Ed, your damned stories are getting more simpleminded every time you tell one. Hell, you dumb hillbillies would drown in five inches of water and call it a deluge."

Edwards retorted, "Just cause you Californys have a strong streak of idiocy don't mean we do. You all heard that the fruits and nuts from all over these here United States have gone to California."

Half listening to Edwards rambling about the great flood, "You know that rushing water and mud took trees, horses, and hundreds of people down the hills...."

Montez broke in, "What are we going to do? I'm going crazy cooped up in this damned base listening to a half-demented fool!"

With his usual aplomb, "I was wondering when you were going to say something intelligent. But to answer your question—let's get the hell outa here."

The villages were off-limits because of encephalitis, an inflammation of the brain transmitted by mosquitoes. At least that was what they were told.

"You know, Ed, I figure mosquitoes can fly for several miles and find you in your bunk as well as shacked up in the village."

"For once you are right. Them there officers in charge of mosquitoes don't want us to have too much fun."

"Yep, and give you something to bitch about." Montez added, "I don't know what you're complaining about—think about those poor bastards living in tents. And the grunts…in the real war. If I had joined the Marines, I'd probably be getting my ass shot off. But you know, sometimes I feel I should be with my buddies and feel just a little guilty."

"Hey, I don't want to hear that old defeatist talk, boy…this is, as they say, 'a Police Action,' not a war. Besides, just be happy that you're not a grunt mucking around in the mud and snow and being shot at for being ugly and being there. Look at those guys that got shot in the air crew. It's the luck of the draw."

They pondered how to escape the confines of the base, the military police, and encephalitis—not to mention the typhoon. To help them think, they sucked on some beer stored in the ammo box under their bunks. It was too early to start drinking beer, but both had to have help on their journey into the "what if we…" to the "it won't work, fool."

Several fellow sufferers trooped in. "Hide the beer," Edwards whispered, "these cabrones will drink us dry!"

The visiting men brought their own liquor. By late afternoon fifteen half-loaded airmen decided to sneak off the base. Then they got serious and eight of them decided upon an excellent plan—they would cut through some small hills and jungle separating them from the village.

Smitty, a mechanic with oil residue in every pore of his skin, said, "It's only about four miles as a bird flies. No sweat GI, this is a snap."

Ike, a fellow crew member, added his wisdom. "You're not a bird. But, if we're going, we got to go now."

"You know," Smitty conceded, "You're right. Hell I can make it in an hour"

Montez leaned over to Edwards and whispered, "You really want to go with these pendejos?"

"Well, they're not too bright, but who is? Except us, of course, and sometimes I wonder about you. Let's give them the benefit of doubt. Besides, those ol' boys will need our guidance."

They decided to only take ten dollars and leave all identification documents and passes at the base. The eight airmen left the base in high spirits, easily going over the perimeter fence. The only real impediment was the howling wind, which seemed to hold them in one place for an interminable length of time, while savagely pelting them with slashing rain, then allowing them to proceed.

The small group finally entered the jungle;

and the wind, still strong enough to bend trees, was diffused by the foliage around them. Deeper into the bush, the air became heavier and their mood no longer light and carefree.

"Goddamn," exclaimed Montez, "keep together or someone's going to get lost." The wind was now muted by the vegetation and trees, and they could hear each others' labored breathing as they pushed their way through the brush. They were sweating profusely and the stifling heat was slowing them down.

Noticing their flagging spirits, Edwards exclaimed, "Not much farther now, guys! I can smell the perfume and booze right up ahead."

When there was no filthy rejoinder from the flagging men, Montez knew something had to give. The point man, Smitty, yelled and grabbed the tall grass and brush around him. He looked down at where he slipped and saw that he nearly fell fifteen feet down into a raging river.

"Jesus Christ, that was a close one. Hear the water down there?" Smitty kept looking down the steep embankment in amazement, "I could have been killed."

"Hell with this, I'm heading back," said one of the men. "Jackson are you going on?"

"I guess I've just about had it. I'm going with you."

Another joined them and three of the group returned to the base. The remaining airmen were now stone sober. Two more hours of thrashing around in the jungle and more of the group headed back. Four men carried on the wayward mission.

Montez knew they were going in the right direction and it would only be a matter of time before they reached the village. They were enveloped in blackness from their shoulders to their sloshy boon Dockers. His skin began to crawl. Luminous, yellow-tinged eyes watched them. He wondered how these creatures' eyes could glow in the dark.

"One of those creatures is following us," Montez yelled to Edwards. "I can tell by the mean eyes."

Ed laughed. "You city boys sure don't know anything about hunting. Why I used to hunt big game at night with my ole hound dog...."

Montez found Ed's monologue comforting that night. He also found it strange and humorous that he was tramping through the jungle in a monsoon just to drink beer and find some girls. No, he thought, it wasn't girls or anything like that. It was the forbidden and the adventure.

"Hey, I thought I saw some lights over yonder," exclaimed Edwards from his higher vantage point. "I really can smell the beer now."

"Yeah, I think I saw...yes, it's the village. Those are houses over there. Hot damn, we made it!"

They stepped up their pace. Montez felt satisfaction that they had not turned back. The trip through the jungle would surely grow in importance and danger as time passed.

When Mamasan saw the first apparition step out of the bush, she screamed, "Aaii, you GI?" and ran inside the house announcing creatures were coming out of nowhere. She returned shortly with Papasan. As they slowly approached them, Montez bowed, "Konbanwa, Mamasan. Konbanwa, Papasan. We need some Nippon biru."

A short time later, villagers crowded around them happy to see airmen with money but disappointed there were only four of them. Serving the thirsty airmen some cold beer, Papasan advised them to keep their voices down and keep out of sight. The Air and Military Police were sweeping all villages near military installations. Edwards and Montez, after a couple of beers, said goodbye to their hosts and started off toward their usual hangout.

Whitey, preening himself, said, "I'm going to find myself some beer and the best poontang in this town… they are going to fight over this ol' country boy."

His buddy, Ike, just grunted and was halfway down the muddy road, looking for the best place in town.

"Hey, Ike, wait for me." Whitey, fatigue forgotten, was in a dead run through the sleeping village trying to catch up to his friend.

The airmen had the village to themselves and enjoyed the attention given. The local businessmen and the girls lost money due to the military putting the towns off-limits; consequently, the airmen's few welcome dollars would buy them more than usual.

Edwards started to loosen up after he inhaled a couple of beers. Two girls appeared from nowhere and sat with them.

"Mamasan, give these gals some beer or whatever they want. How about some music... I feel like country music tonight and to hell with the APs."

Both Mamasan and Papasan tried to convince him that music would surely bring the APs. Mamasan finally quit with,"You crazy GI. Throw in guardhouse. I no care."

"Ed, you have the brains of one of those possums you talk about. Someone should have trapped you before you left those Tennessee hills and joined this here Air Force."

Edwards turned to Mamasan. "This here fella don't understand intelligent, educated folks from the South...he thinks 'Gone with the Wind' has to do with being downwind of an outhouse."

Mamasan walked away shaking her head, "Bacatares," she muttered. "Two foolish ones."

"Well, Ed, what do you think? I'm really enjoying this, but I'm also feeling what we did wasn't too swift."

"Why do you have to analyze everything? We've been enjoying these gals and a couple beers for an hour now. What would we be doing at the barracks?"

"You're right Ed...it's just...we could be

doing something productive. I should be working on my USAFI course homework." Montez added with a grin, "Of course, this gal needs me and that's doing something productive."

"Boy, you've been on those courses for two years now. When you start on advanced algebra, I'll join you. Now let's relax and enjoy."

The straw tatami mats were soft and they were beginning to get a bit sleepy, but they held on. It was only 21:30 hours; the night was young, the beer flowing and the two girls were pretty and eager. Montez thought his girl had the softest lips and soft clear skin. He turned to kiss her again and both heard the sound—the soft wail of a siren, slowly getting stronger as the moments passed. He held his breath and then knew that the damned APs were at it again.

"Get your ass in gear!" Montez yelled. "Let's go out the window. I know where to go."

Edwards went out the window, but he went the wrong way, running straight to the growing fields a few hundred yards away. The villagers called this area their farm, but to Montez it was just a few inches of water full of animal and human feces used to fertilize the soil. The villagers denied that they used "night soil," but Montez came from farm country and had never seen such huge tomatoes and heads of lettuce.

Edwards didn't care. "These here onions and tomatoes are delicious and fit the hamburger buns just right. They never get me sick like our chow."

Montez started after him, yelling, "You're going the wrong way, you idiot!" Too late!

Edwards' body slipped and slid until he went down, butt first into the watery excrement. Montez didn't know whether to laugh or stop running as he looked back at the houses. Suddenly, beams of light like long yellow eyes probed toward their location.

There was only one thing to do. Montez dove into the fetid water, wondering whether to laugh, cry or vomit. Edwards dogpaddled towards him! He looked pathetic, effluvium dripping from his hair and face. Yet he had that look—mischievous, like he was ready to start on some story.

Light beams played on the murky water. "Don't move and shut up." Montez hissed. "Those damn APs won't give up."

As they lay there, barely breathing because of excitement or fear or the bouquet of life around them, Montez remembered a line from Shakespeare: "The rankest compound of villainous smell that ever offended nostril." Old Shakes knew what it was all about.

One of the APs said in disgust, "Jesus Christ, let's get the hell out of here. No one in their right mind would be in that stinking mess."

Finally, the beams of light went out, and they took their first deep breath. Both started to gag. It took a few moments to gain their equilibrium. Edwards tried to gather his wits to say something clever; but when he opened his mouth, he

took in more of the foul water and gave it up.
Miserable, the two sat there for a while, listening as the Jeeps carried their oppressors away.

Montez finally said, "I hope you don't say
anything about this to anyone."

"Monty, this ol' boy may look dumb, but I'm
not completely stupid. Let's get the hell out of
here."

Suddenly they heard yelling and cursing
from the other side of the village. Their two
friends had been caught.

Edwards exclaimed, "We're in free. The cops
got their man and they'll be glad to get out of
here. Poor bastards."

Whitey and Ike were good old boys, Montez
thought. They won't say anything about us.
Peering in the dark, they sloshed through the
muck to the now quiet village. As they came
closer, they began to see some people looking in
their direction—it was Mamasan and some of
the ojosans. The girls giggled as they watched
the two wet men approach, and both airmen
started to breath normally again. When they
were about fifteen feet away, the giggling
changed to shrieks. Montez had forgotten how
they must smell.

Mamasan said, "Follow me, GI. No close.
You smelly too much."

They followed her at a discreet distance until
they came to a long water hose. Mamasan
sprayed them like they were filthy dogs.

"Mamasan," Montez yelled, "The water's

too cold! We can do it ourselves."

"Bacatare GI. Take clothes off." She threw some soap and a brush to them.

Montez and Edwards stood in their skivvies, freezing, while Mamasan picked up their clothes with a stick.

Edwards' teeth chattered. "Mamasan, get us warm and give us some Nippon. I'll give you anything you want."

Without a word, Mamasan stoically handed them some old faded-brown cotton shirts and pants, which they gratefully donned, small and ill-fitting though they were.

Soon they were surrounded by girls, listening to their favorite country and Japanese music, albeit to a rumba beat, and swigging all the beer they could. They felt satisfied that they had outwitted their pursuers. Montez stretched, blissfully comfortable in his favorite spot. He surveyed the small room. Clean tatami mats, familiar Japanese calendars picturing beautiful Japanese girls, and posters hawking the best beers in the Orient. He turned to Edwards who, on the other hand, looked completely out of place—an oversized puppet with his borrowed clothes reaching slightly below the knees and to his elbows.

"Ed, you are about the ugliest thing I've ever seen."

"Boy, what the hell you think you look like?"

Montez noted that Papasan kept a sharp eye out for the police as they danced, sang and generally conducted themselves as two horny GIs would in paradise.

Edwards found a girl with large breasts, his favorite part of the anatomy, as he always did. Every few minutes he would play with them to convince himself that they were real.

Finally, the girl hit him. "You no good GI. No like you pull tittie."

Edwards gladly accepting her blows said, "I say, boy, have you ever in your miserable life thought you would see beauties like these over here?"

Montez agreed, and added, "I tell you, fool, if you pull those tits again, she is going to do you in."

To make amends, Edwards took her back to her little room. "I believe this little gal needs my magnificent body."

The wind still howled outside the wooden structure, every strong gust threatening to knock it over. Montez found the whistling wind and his brief time of alone enjoyable. He inspected the threadbare garb he was wearing and wondered how many years it had been used. He imagined himself to be an Okinawan, living in that house. Looking around the room with new eyes, he saw the little touches the girls must have made: one long-stemmed flower in a thin glass vase in the corner; faded red ribbons holding once white curtains; some old used books on a small table. His Okinawan father taught him to plant rice, sugar cane, sweet potatoes, and soybeans. He worshipped his ancestors and grew up knowing everything would be the same forever.

Montez's reverie was shattered upon Edwards return. Montez sighed, "I hope this sweet repose and rest never stops. They'll just find some skeletons and never know we died with a smile."

After a pause, Edwards said, "You know it's going to be a bitch getting back to the base with these here winds a howling all around us…unless we go back the same way we got here."

"You pendejo," Montez exclaimed. "Why do you have to bring up getting back to the base…I just started having fun and you go ruin it all."

His partner was right. He had been concerned for over an hour about how they would get back to the base. But he'd never let Edwards know that—Edwards would torture him unmercifully for months. Montez knew how they would get back, but he wanted Edwards to stew for a while.

Edwards didn't pursue the question. He knew Montez would do all the fretting. With heavy heart, and some trepidation, the two men said their goodbyes and began their journey back to the base.

Edwards looked out the window. "Oh Christ, looks like the monsoon is done…only heavy rain and wind. Our cover is gone."

"Damn, we should have noticed," said Montez, donning his poncho. "Just looks like a squall now… the APs can see us."

Montez hired a pedicab, and the two airmen hid on the floor of the small cab, arms and legs entwined. "Damn, we should have taken a couple of brews with us to whet our appetite."

"My God, you just finished eating an hour ago. But you're right, I'm hungry as a horse."

As they drew close to the main gate, the two men sprinted into the boondocks. It was easy. They just walked through the bush, climbed over some fences, and were inside the base. Triumphantly, they reached their barracks ready to expound on their magnificent trek through the wilds and the properly expanded debauchery that followed.

Unfortunately, their sergeant had already heard of their exploits. They were confined to the barracks for being AWOL.

"Monty, I think we stepped into it this time. That old boy was not too happy with us."

"Don't sweat it, Ed, as soon as the storm recedes we'll be needed on the flight line to get the plane ready… and will be home free."

They felt better when the men heard they were back and crowded the room. Soon they, including the ungrateful sergeant who put them in confinement, attentively listened to their exaggerated trip exploits.

"During our hike in the jungle," Montez modestly told them, "I had to throw rocks and pieces of branches at wild animals to keep them from attacking us. As Ed knows, I led the guys through the storm and it wasn't easy, I tell ya."

Edwards, without missing a beat chimed in, "Yeah, he was the point man. You know he has lots of Injun blood, even more than me, and we can find any trail. It's in our blood."

"The only reason we came back so soon was our sense of duty. We knew that the storm was ending and we'd be needed to keep our boys flying."

That was for the sergeant's sake. The assembled airmen groaned, and the two heroes finished with how they outwitted the combined might of the Air Police, the Military Police, and for good measure, the Shore Patrol.

Edwards put it into perspective by explaining, "Ya'll are heroes in this here war, but we peons must also humbly serve by keeping the home fires burning and damned if we didn't do us all proud."

The typhoon receded in a couple of days and, as expected, they returned to the flight line as soon as their plane returned with dire warnings by the sergeant about being caught pissing in the wrong place.

Montez told Edwards, "You know, it was dumb what we did. We were lucky not to get into trouble."

"Hell, boy, I know that. Next time I'll do it the right way. I just don't like that there fertilizer they use. But don't you worry, son, yore daddy'll take care of you."

Montez smiled. "I don't know who's taking care of us, but I hope they don't stop."

Chapter 5

Shelby

Everyone agreed that Shelby was the ugliest man in the world with a most improbable name. Only twenty-three-years-old, he walked like a man fifteen years older. His bland rusty-brown hair grew in wispy tufts, covering balding spots with lifeless oily-looking strands. Although he was as tall as Montez at six feet, stooped bony shoulders diminished his frame. The khaki uniform hanging loosely on his gaunt body further accentuated Shelby's pale skin and washed-out appearance.

Montez and Edwards first met Shelby by accident at the supply shack near the flight line while securing aircraft parts for their B-29 bomber. They walked into the darkened building from a bright island sun and found nine airmen waiting for the clerk nearest the entrance. A sad-sack looking airman at the far corner of the long counter wasn't busy, so they went to him; their eyes still adjusting to the dimness of the room. After a few words, they knew why everyone was lined up at the first counter. This clerk's face was covered with zits — not normal, everyday, young man's zits, but red, open sores on his cheeks, forehead, nose and some larger pustules on his neck that looked like they continued down his shoulders and back. The zits overlaid skin left marked by childhood chicken pox, fighting for space with the short, porcine bristles scattered over his cheeks and chin. His teeth matched his face: brown-stained stumps in front, flanked by long yellow incisors that stretched his thin lips.

Montez tried to look above and to one side. No use. His gaze was drawn to this apparition. At last, they finished their order! They tried to rush out, but the clerk stopped them to give instructions on a new module.

As Montez and Edwards edged out of the supply room, the persistent clerk followed. "I've only been here for a few weeks, and I really enjoy Okinawa. My name is Shelby. What's yours?"

Montez opened his mouth to reply, but Shelby went on. "I guess you guys really must work hard. I know that the Pesky Fly has had more missions over Korea than any other B-29. I keep track of such things. I guess I'm just a twenty-year man."

During this monologue, Edwards kept muttering, "Dang, is that right? Jesus Christ! Gotta go."

Montez was speechless. He knew Shelby wanted to talk; he could hear the pleading in his voice. Edwards also sensed it. "Let's get together sometime," he suggested. "We'll show you around."

"That's great!" Shelby answered. "I went to town once but returned right away. When do you want to go? I can go after work…or anytime you can get away."

Montez and Edwards promised they would get hold of him and then tripped over each other to get out of there.

"Ed, you idiot! Now we're stuck with that guy. Every time I let you talk, you screw things up. I oughta send you back to those dumb hills where you come from."

Montez berated Edwards all the way back to the aircraft. He felt sorry for Shelby too and was also going to ask him to join them sometime, but he would never let Edwards know about it. Edwards was going to pay for being overly friendly, not him.

❖❖❖❖❖

Their first meeting with Shelby was at the base movie house, a large gray warehouse type of building, bustling with servicemen lined up to buy tickets. While waiting, they studied the wives and daughters of the officers and their civilian counterparts, rating their appearance from 1 to 10.

"Lawd have mercy! Monty, look at that

brown-haired girl with those big ole bazookas. She's a 9 if I ever saw one!" Edwards was a tit-man through and through. He knew every name ever used in the English language for breasts and then some. He was ecstatic over them, even quoting from the "Song of Solomon."

"She's only a 6 and that is being generous, as I'm known to be," replied Montez. "Only reason you're panting like a goddamned dog is because of her boobs." For good measure Montez added, "I take you out of those damned hills in Tennessee, but no one can take the hills out of your warped mind."

Before Edwards could reply, Shelby walked towards them. His uniform was newly laundered and stiff, but Shelby with his sunken chest and narrow boy shoulders still looked like a scarecrow. In front of the lighted theater, the two airmen got a better look at Shelby's features. His countenance had not improved, particularly his teeth, which were crooked, yellow and open-spaced as an old man's.

"He looks like Boris Karloff," Montez whispered. "No, he's uglier than Karloff!"

Edwards agreed softly, "Ya know, Monty, I think he's even uglier than you and that's saying a lot."

All eyes seemed to be on the three of them, and Montez felt self-conscious. He hated himself for feeling that way and tried to make up for it with a loud greeting. Then he felt foolish for being so noisy. The normally talkative Edwards was at a loss for words but quickly recovered by putting a friendly hand on Shelby's shoulder.

What distressed Montez the most were Shelby's grey eyes — large, lustrous, and topped by fanned lashes — sad eyes, so melancholy it hurt to look into them. It was impossible to look at him casually, to see that gargoyle face with its incongruous eyes. A broad grin spread over Shelby's face. Montez wished he would stop smiling. It gave Shelby's face a satanic appearance.

"Hey boy, where you been?" Edwards said. "We've been here waiting for a coon's age." That broke the ice. As they moved into the theatre, they all started talking at once.

"I heard this is a good movie," said Montez.

"Yeah, I heard it is," Edwards agreed, trying to think of something else to say.

"We better hurry and get some seats — it's crowded." Montez pushed Edwards forward until they sat down. The movie mercifully started immediately.

After the movie, Shelby talked about his life — how his mother died; his stepmother who disliked him; his siblings who not only disliked him, but were ashamed of him. He talked for an hour straight. Finally, Montez asked the question he had running through his mind ever since Shelby insisted on paying for the movie. He had more script in his wallet than Montez had seen all year.

"I know this may sound nosy, but are you

rich or something. You know paying for us. I couldn't help noting all that script in your wallet? Not that I'm complaining."

Shelby explained that he came from a rich family, lived in one of those affluent little towns in Massachusetts, and had a degree in economics from Amherst College.

Edwards quickly found a solution for a rich boy. "We're going to show you the town. I know a musume — 'girl' to you, son, who will really go for you."

He turned to Montez, "We are going to take this ol' boy under our tutelage, feed, and breed him proper until he runs out of that nasty ol' money." Shelby just grinned.

Eventually, they got used to Shelby's upper-crust Eastern accent, even that broad "A" sound. But they could not stand the way he enunciated his words so perfectly. In a world of uneducated young men, this "affliction" only alienated him further.

"Boy," Edwards said one day, "You just got to shape up and quit talking funny. Try to talk like a good ol' boy — like an American...like me."

"God almighty, don't talk like that dumb hillbilly," Montez cut in. "But you got to quit using those big words when you're around Ed's friends and the other guys. It's making us look bad."

Shelby looked at them dumbfounded. "You mean I don't speak correctly? Everybody in this outfit has a different accent or way of speaking. What's wrong with the way I communicate?"

"That's the problem," Montez replied. "You do speak correctly. No one else does; and you, well, tend to stand out. For example, Ed has an accent, but all dumb hillbillies talk that way and no one pays attention."

Edwards sent him an injured look. "Ah taught this here wetback the King's English, and he still has a Rio Grande accent!"

Shelby broke in. "Well, I still feel that I speak like everyone else, but with just a slight New England dialect. Besides I notice that both of you speak differently, use different words, when you're alone discussing religion and philosophy. I heard you discussing the contradictions of Thomas Malthus and David Ricardo. In any case, I'm going to send for some books by the worldly philosophers and some writings by a new fellow named John Galbraith and his theory of competing oligopolies."

The two sergeants looked at each other. Shelby was really smart, Montez thought, but he seemed to lack the common touch. Perhaps he'd had so little contact with just plain folks that he was out of step.

Shelby had joined the service as an enlisted man "just to see the world, get away from home for awhile and see how I fit in." Later he confessed that he joined to get away from parents and relatives who were ashamed of him and gave him nothing but money so he could travel.

He finally came to terms with himself and didn't care what people thought.

Montez thought that Shelby should have been an officer, and he wanted to ask him why he didn't use some of his money to get plastic surgery or do something about his teeth. But he just couldn't do it—maybe later.

Shelby continued, "You know that I'm not complaining about my parents... actually, my father and stepmother. They gave me everything I wanted. It's just that they were always gone."

Montez nodded his head in sympathy. He also had a stepmother he'd just as soon forget.

Shelby lived at the library and its books. "I couldn't stay at home because no one was there except the servants. So you guys weren't the only ones that lived in books."

"Now lookee here boy," Edwards broke in, "I went to the library 'cause there were some fine women there. No servants ever bothered me none." His face lit up, "I bet you even had some nice upstairs maids to take care of every whim yore little ol' mind could think of."

"Don't listen to that horny bastard," interjected Montez. "He'll corrupt your mind and soul. But did you really have maids? Young, pretty ones?"

Shelby shook his head, "Christ, you guys really can't imagine how formal everything was. We hardly ever talked to the servants unless we wanted something done."

Over time, Shelby told them his entire story,

and Montez and Edwards took him officially under their wings.

Edwards put it succinctly, "That ol' boy needs looking after and so does his money."

Their first trip to the village with Shelby was memorable. They rented a bicycle cab, and Shelby chattered excitedly all the way to the village. "You know, the first and only time I went to town was an unmitigated disaster. None of the girls came up to me; some were making fun of me. I resolved never to go to the village again... but here I am."

Plaintively he asked, "Do you think that the girl will like me? What if she already has a boyfriend? Maybe, I'll just take it easy and not expect too much. How much farther is this place?"

"Hey, orale vato loco!" Montez blurted. "Play it cool, we have all night." Montez liked to show off his barrio slang, even if he didn't know what a lot of it really meant.

Hanging on to the bouncing pedicab, Montez observed that both Edwards and Shelby took to Mexican slang immediately. Shelby was hilarious in his Boston accent. "'Vato pendejo.' I believe that is the correct phrase, is it not?"

As was his custom, Shelby read a book on Spanish fundamentals and was quite good at it, albeit with a Boston accent. Edwards was unintelligible when he spoke. He mixed up his put-on hillbilly accent with Mexican slang and a new language appeared. Montez believed he did it on purpose because Edwards could mimic any accent or language.

Shelby saw the village first. "Orale, ese. I think I see it. Oh boy, I just saw some girls slip into that little house!" Edwards tried to calm him down before he damaged himself. They finally got off the rickety cab safely and sauntered toward their favorite watering hole.

"Shelby, now goddamn, you behave yourself with these here musumes or I won't let you buy me anymore beer," Edwards admonished. They sat down on a porch-like stoop, worn shiny by countless young men, and ordered Nippon beer. It was an excellent location. They could see the GIs coming and going with their girls and later gaze at the sunset.

Seven bottles of beer apiece later, Montez and Edwards contentedly watched the still-bright sun setting in a multihued sky. Shelby was finally talking to one of the girls. They couldn't find Mariko, the girl they promised him. Shelby didn't seem to mind too much, until his current girl meandered off to another GI.

"Damn," muttered Edwards. "That gal just took off on Shelby...I'm going to get my money back."

"What do you mean get your money back?"

Edwards started towards the girl. "I gave that mu-sume two bucks to get together with Shelby."

"For Christ's sake, Ed, sit down. You have to let him go at it by himself, or he'll never learn."

Montez led him by the arm to a morose Shelby.

Edwards slapped Shelby on the back to cheer him up. "You can't let some old musume scare you off. Besides I know you will really like Mariko."

"But do you think she will like me? That's the question."

"Boy, you leave it to your old uncle Ed. I can tell you that gal won't keep her hands off you."

"Mariko is really a nice girl, not like the ones you've met," Montez added, ordering another round of beer. He hoped for some miracle to save the night.

Mariko finally appeared, to their immense relief, and was introduced to a reluctant Shelby. Mariko was no looker—short, two or three inches under five feet, squat, moonfaced with tiny slits for eyes and a stub nose. But her quick smile revealed even white teeth, and a sunny disposition. Like Shelby, she found it hard to find "friends" of the opposite sex, which was calamitous in her profession.

She looked at Shelby with some trepidation, "Hello, GI, you want biru, ne? My name Mariko." After introducing herself, she brought him a beer, and then fell silent, stealing glances at him as if she couldn't believe her eyes.

"That's a pretty name. I'm Shelby and this is my first time here."

Their conversation picked up enough so that Montez and Edwards felt comfortable leaving them alone. "Son, I feel we've done our duty, and it's time for this little old country boy to get some action."

"Ed, I saw some really pretty girls walking just outside the village on the main road, but I...."

"Mamasan, two birus for the road, dozo." Edwards' long legs were already in motion. "I say boy. You just going to sit there looking ugly?"

Edwards was off! It didn't matter that he didn't know where the girls were; he was always on the prowl.

Montez finished his beer, grabbed a full cold Nippon and sauntered after him in the setting sun. He saw Edwards talking with three girls on the main road leading to the village. Something didn't look right. Those girls were not dressed like the girls they were used to. And they had an uncomfortable look on their faces. These were "cherry girls" as the GIs called them. Not prostitutes.

Edwards was his usual self—he didn't care if they were from the moon. They were girls, and he was doing his best to convince them to go out with him. The girls were trying to explain, in broken English, that they couldn't go out with him; they were good girls.

Montez caught up to them. "You dumb hillbilly, don't you know we could get in trouble? These are cherry girls!"

"Why, hell, boy. You just look here at these

musu-mes. They're the prettiest gals I've seen in a coon's age."

Edwards was trying out his best Southern accent for the girls, but they didn't seem impressed. The girls were pretty, with delicate features, slim bodies, and shiny black hair. One of them kept looking at Edwards with a nice smile. Montez decided to jump in. Might as well have some fun if they were going to get into trouble anyway. Who knows, maybe they'd get lucky.

Finally, talking and pleading with the girls for an hour, two of the girls agreed to see them at a beach near their hometown of Nago in a few days.

Edwards was beside himself. "See, you uneducated wetback! Your Uncle Ed takes care of things. I get you women, buy you booze, and teach you to be a good American." Shaking his head, he added sadly, "An you don't 'preciate it."

They laughed and joked all the way back. Shelby and Mariko had hit it off; and Edwards and Montez had dates, tentative though they might be, with real live girls. Montez knew it could lead to trouble with parents and the local community if they weren't careful, but it didn't dampen his mood. The dusty, warm road back to the village seemed shorter; the wooden shacks with their droopy red and yellow banners didn't look as run down as they had earlier in the day. In reality, the village had an impoverished look and feel with only a minimum of comfort for its inhabitants, who were mostly female. Whatever frills available were there because the GIs expected them.

They got close enough to the village to smell the manure and fresh-tilled earth scent, mixed with the odor of beer, sake, and cheap perfume. With a few beers, the smell, the drab view, and the noise level gradually became tolerable. The loneliness Montez felt, especially when he saw the hot red ball of the setting sun, also became tolerable. As the darkening shadows gauzed the scabs, concealing the shabbiness and purpose of their surroundings, forgetfulness set in. The girls became merrier and miraculously prettier.

Edwards broke into Montez's reverie, "Well, hot damn. Look at old Shelby! He looks happier than a pig in slop."

Sure enough, Shelby and Mariko were still talking, their heads touching, oblivious of anyone else in the noisy restaurant.

"This boy's in love!" Montez joked to Edwards. "He looks like he wants to get wed, not in bed."

"Don't they look nice together... just like prom night."

"For Christ's sake Ed, they had proms where you're from? Even if they did, you didn't have clean clothes to wear."

Edwards, however, would not be deterred. "Ah just knew they were going to be thick as thieves, just look at them."

"One hour to get back to the base," Montez reminded Shelby.

Shelby turned to them with a huge smile. Mariko's pumpkin face looked absolutely cherubic, and her large gold tooth gleamed.

"Shelbysan nice GI!" she proclaimed. "He no touchie. He nice to Mariko. Wakarimaska?"

"We understand," said Montez. "He's ichiban. You take care of number one boy."

They waited for Shelby to say goodbye. Edwards surprised Montez by speaking with his serious voice. "I'm a little concerned with that old boy. He's a little too tied up with that musume. He could get his ass in the wringer and not be able to get out."

"Come on, Ed. Who do you think you are, his father? Let's go check out those musumes that just walked in." Montez also had some misgivings, but he tried to forget them as they made conversation with the new girls.

Finally, they pried Shelby away from Mariko and started back to the base. Shelby was strangely quiet. After several questions went unanswered, he said, "I have never talked to a girl like I did tonight. I just like her. And I think she likes me. I'm going to see her tomorrow night and...."

Edwards cut in, "Boy, you just take it easy. You know she is just a good time gal, and she knows a lot of guys just like you. Wakarimaska?"

"I know what she is. I'm not blind. She didn't

deny it and wouldn't if she could. I'm going to see her when she's not working and go to the beach."

Montez and Edwards knew they were going to have a problem.

"You know that Ed is not too bright," Montez said to Shelby. "You can tell by the flat spots on his face he got from bumping into trees. But he does know a little about women and the trouble they cause. Even more important, do what I tell you and you can't go wrong." Shelby just smiled that smile, and didn't say anything.

❖❖❖❖❖

The air war was winding down. United Nations troops were deep into North Korea, and the airmen figured the powers-that-be would let them go home early. Montez and Edwards hadn't been to the village for two weeks but didn't care. They'd work every night straight if it helped send them home. They knew that Shelby was with Mariko every night he could.

Then everything changed. The Air Force Times reported that the Chinese crossed the 38th parallel and were pushing the United Nations' troops down the Korean peninsula.

"Well, I guess we're going to be here for a lot longer than I figured," groused Montez as he jumped into the truck heading for the flight line.

Their bomber racked up missions on a driving schedule but had been lucky so far. Shrapnel damage was extensive, but no real harm had come to the aircraft or aircrew.

"Look at this big ol' hole near where Fromer sits. Missed his ass by just a foot."

"Christ, look at this cluster of holes on the wing," replied Montez. "These missions to the Yalu River sure pick up the flack. Just lucky none of our crew was hit."

A loud explosion came from the tail section of the plane. Montez and the rest of the crew dropped their tools and ran towards the rear of the aircraft. They found Sergeant Johnson, the rear gunner, sprawled on the tarmac, as if taking a nap, a pool of blood slowly growing around his head. A metal plate now stuck to where his face had been. The dumbfounded men milled helplessly around their friend's body, then walked to the front of their ship to guide the shrieking ambulance to the body. Later working on the aircraft, a shaken Montez and Edwards talked about how Johnson's screwdriver must have slipped and the back plate of the twenty caliber machine gun exploded in his face. He was either too tired or grew careless in his haste to get to debriefing.

Montez stared at the area where Johnson fell. It was still wet from the hosing down by firemen. "He didn't have a chance…he was dead before he hit the ground." Montez added, "It's hard to think of him dead. I just talked to him a few hours ago, and he had big plans for tonight."

"Yeah, he complained to me about the holes in his lunch box," Edwards said. "Like the rest of the air crew, he believed a rat was in the plane eating their food. Poor bastard."

A truck pulled up in front of their aircraft to give the crew a ride to the barracks. Trudging to the truck, Montez asked himself and Edwards, "How could a rat live in the plane at those altitudes—over 33,000 feet? We would have found dropping or something in the cabins or the tunnel." He added, "The rat would have to live in the wings or some other unpressurized part of the plane."

"Think about it." Edwards mused. "He was killed after completing at least ten missions—not by flack or MiGs, but here—safe, in front of us."

"I don't want to think or talk about it," replied Montez, happy to be speeding away from the scene. Johnson hadn't been a buddy, but he was a nice guy and shouldn't have gone that way.

The following morning, they talked about Shelby and the mythical rat. They hadn't seen Shelby for three weeks. They knew he was going to the village every day he could and laughed off their concern.

Montez said, "You know, I think we feel guilty about Shelby's forays into the unknown. After all, we introduced him to the flesh pots of the island."

"Hell, I don't feel guilty," replied Edwards, pulling away the yellow metal and wood platform from the engine. "If anything, I'm jealous he's having a good time and we're here."

They tried to forget about the dates they made and couldn't keep with the two beautiful girls they met on the road. Then their plane caught some heavy flack and was diverted to an airbase in Japan. They bet that the flight crew made every excuse to divert to Japan for a little fun.

They went looking for Shelby at their favorite hangout and were told that he and Mariko were out on a date! A date, just like in the States! Instead of their usual carousing in the village, they grabbed a pedicab and set out for Nago to find the cherry girls. They found Nago to have some industry, stores, and well-built red-tile-roof houses. They walked around for an hour to get the lay of the land, then got thirsty for Nippon beer and hungry for soba, the ubiquitous noodle soup. Both of them felt uneasy in this village—it wasn't geared for carousing GIs—and decided to head for the nearest beach, only a few minutes away by pedicab.

When they arrived, Edwards let out a holler. "There they are! Boy, are they sweet looking and waiting for this ol' county boy!"

The girls didn't even acknowledge his greeting, but Montez knew that old Ed would take care of things. His trust was fulfilled in a short period of time. For future reference and revenge, Montez noted that Edwards immediately commandeered the prettier one named Jun; but Montez thought his date, Kimiko, had more class, and he let Edwards know about it repeatedly.

"Kimiko, you know Ed is a philanderer." He got her attention with that word. She did not know what it meant, but it sounded important.

"He inherited some kind of a disease. He goes from one girl to another with no regard for their feelings. His father and all his male relatives have it."

Montez finally convinced Edwards that Kimiko had more class than his girl and wouldn't be interested in a no-class guy like him. Knowing Edwards couldn't pass up the challenge, Montez kept it up until he couldn't resist. In short order, Edwards started to weave his legendary charm on Kimiko.

Kimiko listened to Edward's blarney for a while, her dark eyes flashing daggers, and then coldly told him, "You talk talk all time. You no good GI…go to many ojosan."

"Hey, Ed, how come you can't leave girls alone? You notice that my girl knows I don't fool around. You better do something or you're out in the cold."

"Monty, you did it. I know you did it."

Afterwards, Edwards apologized to both girls for his faux pas and all was forgiven. They went swimming and boating in water so clear you could see at least thirty feet down to an ocean floor covered with multi-colored rocks and hundreds of different sizes and colors of fish. Montez rubbed two coral rocks together causing scores of small canary-yellow fish, some with black markings making the yellow color more brilliant, to swarm around him consuming the powdery debris.

Later, as the men relaxed on the warm white sand, Montez contemplated, while drinking his cold beer, on how life was sweet to those who attempted the forbidden.

Then he noticed that someone was blocking his sun, but before he could look around, Edwards drawled, "I think we have uninvited guests, and there's a potful of them."

Montez saw five young Okinawan men staring hard at them and the girls. No one said anything. Then Kimiko suddenly starting rattling off Japanese at them; and they answered sullenly, but forcefully, what sounded like accusations.

"Ed, I think we should get up slowly just in case these cabrones jump us."

"Monty, watch that one on the left; he's circling around!"

Montez studied the young men. They looked like fishermen in their early twenties, with heavily tanned skin, faded denim trousers cut just below the knee, and loose blue cotton skirts. A tall, muscular Okinawan standing forward and center of the group had the bearing of the leader. He also had the most ferocious look on his face. After a few moments, Montez bowed slightly, "Konnichiwa. Eigo wo hanase masu ka?"

There was no answer from the young men,

only a look of surprise on their faces.

"Sumimasen, eigo no dekiru hito wa ima-suka…."

Edwards broke in, "What the hell you saying…?"

"Quiet Ed, I'm trying to…."

One of the young men slipped forward, brusquely injecting, "I speak English. What do you want here?"

Montez replied, "We're just visiting this beautiful beach and talking to these nice girls we just met."

"Iie. Go away now. Hayaku!"

Looking at Edwards, Montez quietly said, "Let's go, while the getting is good."

Turning to the men and again bowing slightly, "Wakirimashita. Gomenasai."

The spokesman said something to Michiko, and then the men retreated a few feet, stopped, and curiously looked at the two airmen as they gathered their belongings.

Michiko quickly told them to leave. Montez and Edwards obliged them with slow movements, just to let the world know they weren't being run off.

While buttoning his shirt, Edwards pleaded with Jun for another date, but this time somewhere far in the future. The girls quickly agreed, although Montez believed they did so just to get them out of there. They made a quiet but dignified withdrawal.

As they left the beach area looking for a pedicab,

Edwards asked, "What the hell did you say? You sounded like one of those goddamned gooks. Where did you pick up their lingo. I think you've gone completely Asiatic."

"Take it easy, ridge-runner. I just saved your ass from a well-deserved kicking." Montez added, "All I asked, I think, is if they could speak English, excused myself and said good afternoon." He added, after a moment, "You know, this is their turf—we really don't belong."

Edwards was still in a state of disbelief, looking at his friend as if he were seeing him for the first time, "Damn, if you didn't sound just one of like them...bowing and all that stuff."

"You know I've been practicing Japanese and it's easy. I pronounce it like Spanish and it comes out perfectly."

"Well, I'll be goddamned!"

On their way to their watering hole in a pedicab to look for Shelby, they started the inevitable recitation of how they could have taken them if they really had to.

"Good thing those guys backed off before we beat the shit out of them. But you looked ridiculous trying to get your long bony legs in your pants before they jumped us," said Montez.

Edwards growled, "Hell boy, I could've licked those gooks all by my lonesome."

Of course, they both knew they would have gotten their asses kicked.

They arrived just in time to see Shelby and Mariko walking hand-in-hand on the long dusty road back to the village. The bearing of Shelby's tall, bony body gave the impression that he was trying to convince Mariko to do something. Marico's short, thick body and nodding head, gave the appearance of acceptance. All in all, it was a sight to behold.

After greeting them, Montez commented softly, "At least he looks happy and has someone to share it with while we spend our time chasing musumes nearly getting our ass kicked and bitching."

"What you say, Monty? Quit yore mumbling boy and stand tall."

Montez wistfully replied, "Look how happy Shelby is. I wish I could find someone I liked like that."

"Boy, you've been here too long. Yeah, he looks happy; but hell, I need some round eyes to get me happy."

Montez snorted, "Hell, I've seen better looking horses than those gals in the pictures you showed me. Christ, one of them even had a pipe, with a long stem, in her mouth! And I bet they even paid you to screw them."

Chapter 6

The Wedding

In high spirits when they got to the village to pick up Shelby, Montez ordered some beer. Montez saw Shelby and Mariko at their usual table — their heads together, whispering conspiratorily, oblivious to the tipsy GIs and the chattering girls around them. They were holding hands, fingers intertwined, like lovers throughout the world. Montez felt as if he were intruding when he broke up the conversation.

"Let's go, Shelby, or we're going to get our asses in the wringer." To Montez's surprise, Shelby kissed Mariko goodbye and walked to the restaurant's entrance before Montez had a chance to finish his beer.

As they bumped their way to the base in a pedicab, Shelby said quietly, "I want you guys to hear me out and not say anything until I finish. I asked Mariko to be my wife, and she accepted my proposal. We're getting married in two months." And in the same matter of fact voice he added, "Monty, I want you to be my best man."

Montez just stared at Shelby, then at Edwards, waiting for someone to start laughing or make some stupid remark about anything.

Finally, Edwards exclaimed, "I know you're bull-shitting us. But you know you almost made me believe it." He was so surprised, he forgot to exaggerate his hillbilly drawl.

"Believe it," Shelby replied in a curt voice.

Montez saw that Shelby was dead serious. "Why, sure, I'll be best man...but first let's talk about this."

Shelby thanked him and sat silent.

In an unusually serious voice, Edwards said, "You know the Air Force won't let you get married if they get wind of this...they might not even let you off the base or transfer you."

Montez knew he had to dissuade him, or at least try. "Shelby, she is a prostitute. Do you have any idea what is ahead of you if you carry this out?"

Edwards added, "Yeah, she's a one-time girl. What are you going to do when her regulars meet up with you all? Discuss the last time?"

Shelby answered in a soft voice. "Next time you say anything like that about Mariko, I'm going to kick your ass. She is going to be my wife no matter what."

Montez just sat, dumbfounded. He had never heard Edwards speak that way to Shelby. And Shelby...!

"Ed just said what everyone will be saying. Mariko is a prostitute and always will be to GIs. Who knows what the Okinawans are going to think or say? Besides how can you be in love? You just met her. You don't know anything about her."

"How do you know how long it takes to fall in love? Do you have to see her ten times or maybe eighty? I know she's a prostitute and an Oriental, but that doesn't change things."

Montez shifted uncomfortably and looked at Shelby's sad eyes. "We won't say anything else about her. We're your friends, whether you believe it or not. I can't understand your reasoning or why you want to do this, but we'll back you up."

"Yeah, we'll back you," added Edwards. "I'm sorry about what I said, but you probably would have said the same thing if one of us were marrying one of our old musumes. You'd think we're crazy."

After a minute of silence, Shelby raised his head and squared his bony shoulders. "You guys don't know how it feels to be so ugly that people turn their heads. You don't get up from bed and look at yourself in the mirror every damn morning and know people are going to stare at you in disbelief." He blinked away the wetness in his eyes and took a long breath. "You think I don't know? You think I'm blind or dumb? You think I can't see my ugly...no, grotesque features. My repugnant skin? God, I wish I were blind and dumb."

Montez and Edwards looked away from him in silence. Shelby continued with a passion in his voice they had never imagined. "You berate me for wanting to marry this girl whom you call a gook and a whore. I call her darling and she loves me for what I am inside. She was honest; and yes, told me I was ugly — in her words 'not pretty boy.' But she also said I was gentle and nice. That I had the spirit of a beautiful bird and even saw beauty in my eyes and in me. Yes, I'll marry her and damn you all."

Montez swallowed hard and in a quiet voice said, "No matter what you think of us for saying what we thought, we're still your buddies. If you really want us to leave you alone, we will."

Edwards laid his arm around Shelby's shoulder. "We're your friends and we wouldn't give a damn if you went AWOL or got married. And, old boy, if you do it, you are going to need friends."

Shelby calmed down and a smile lit up his gargoyle face. "Thanks, you guys. I know that you're probably the only friends that I have. I also know that you think you're helping me. Yes, I'm asking you to be my friends and to help me if I need it."

Montez and Edwards let out a collective sigh of relief. Montez turned toward Shelby, put his arm on his shoulders and said, "We'll help, old buddy, but don't get mad at us if we continue to have doubts and even try to change your mind."

At the base, they continued discussing the pros and cons of the wedding. Shelby calmly listened and had a logical answer to each of their objections. He and Mariko had been discussing these problems for over a month, and they both knew what the military could do. They didn't care. They would get married by a civilian minister or a monk in the Okinawan tradition.

Shelby informed them, "My attorney will handle the legal aspects of the marriage." Montez and Edwards shook their heads in disbelief—Shelby and Mariko had been discussing the wedding for over a month, and they didn't even have an inkling of it.

The news spread throughout the base and to military installations miles away. Apparently Mariko's friends couldn't keep quiet, and nearly the entire population knew about the marriage of a soldier and a bar girl. Montez and Edwards continued to spend days and nights trying to talk Shelby out of it, to no avail. Shelby was in love and nothing his two friends could say or do could change his mind. Finally, they gave in.

"All right, you stupid son-of-a-bitch," exclaimed a frazzled Edwards. "We'll help you, if we can."

"What do you want us to do? Montez added.

Montez had never seen Shelby so happy. "I knew you guys would help me."

Edwards, back in form, said, "We're going to have you a wedding like no one's seen in this here island. You just leave it to us, boy, but keep yore cash handy."

Edwards invited every hillbilly friend he had at the airbase. Montez got all of his Chicano friends to come. They decided to have both country music and romantic Mexican boleros for dancing. They could stand each other's music for one night. Besides, the Rebel yell and the Mexican grito were cool. They had misgivings, but their air and ground crew, as well as other friends, promised to be there.

The one person in Montez's ground crew who felt strongly about the marriage was assistant crew chief Easley. "Goddamn Yankee bastard. Going to have some half breed gooks — mark my words. Mongrelizing the white race, that's what they do."

No one paid much attention to him, but Montez knew that most of his friends thought like Easley and worried they would cause trouble at the marriage ceremony.

Shelby was the only calm person. He didn't offer suggestions. He answered their questions with, "You guys act like you're the ones getting married! You are doing everything I would do, so do it!"

Edwards was like an old mother hen, double-checking everything they did. "Monty, did you finish the list of guys invited? What about a cake? Do you have the Monk set up?"

"Ed, quit your damn questions and simmer down. You spend more time running around asking questions than doing anything useful!"

When Edwards announced, "We're going to dress in light blue tuxedos, just like guys in wedding parties in Nashville. I'm also partial to tails…you know, those things that hang from your suit coat?"

At that, Shelby finally stepped in. "Ed, I don't think that tuxedos or tails will look good at an Okinawan wedding." Fortunately, there were no tuxedos in Okinawa, light blue or otherwise.

Later Edwards got another fertile idea. "I'm gonna get me some swords, and Shelby can have a full military wedding. We can have our crew hold them old swords over their heads, and they can walk under them just like in the movies."

Montez was too startled to say anything! Visions of their ground crew with Samurai swords flashed through his mind. My God! Sergeant Easley with a sword. He could hardly use a wrench without dropping it on someone's head! "Ed, I talked to Shelby about how fancy he wanted the wedding," he lied. "He said that he wanted it to be simple. He doesn't want to hurt your feelings, but he wants it simple."

Edwards was disappointed, "I understand how he wouldn't want it too fancy, but how many weddings do you have here?"

Montez took a deep breath. "You know, Ed, we could wear our class A uniforms and pin a white flower on our blouses to show the formality of the situation." Reluctantly, Edwards accepted the inevitable.

Mariko was in a state of confusion. Montez asked her several times if she had invited her girlfriends. Finally, with an enigmatic, moon-faced smile she said, "No sweat, everybody come. Tokusan ojosans — lots of girls, ne. Many numba one girls come."

Montez tried to discuss the ceremony and its potential problem with Shelby, who wouldn't talk about it. Montez refused to let it go.

"At least think about where you're going to live! What if the Air Force transfers you back to the States? What if you get Mariko pregnant and then you have to leave right away?"

Shelby looked at Montez, appeared to make up his mind and said, "All right Monty, I was saving this as a surprise, but I already bought a house not too far from the base, but far enough where we don't get the normal GI traffic. I transferred enough funds so that Mariko can live comfortably the rest of her life. Now, will you leave me alone for awhile?"

Montez stared at him as if seeing him clearly for the first time. "When did you do all that? I mean how did you manage to do…."

"Christ's sake, it wasn't difficult. I have a lawyer in Boston — he did it all, including buying and transferring the property to my name and to Mariko. It helps to have money. Sometimes it makes life easier."

"Well I'll be damned! Wait till I tell Ed, he won't believe it."

While helping plan the ceremony, Montez

became interested in Okinawan religious beliefs — an Animist religion based on reverence for fire and hearth and worship of their ancestors. He and an unenthusiastic Edwards visited the large womb-like cement tombs, holding the Okinawan ancestors' remains in urns, scattered throughout the island. Montez always looked for a way to get inside of the tombs, but they appeared to be solid concrete.

Mariko would not tell Montez or Edwards much about her religion. Perhaps she had none. Nor would she tell them about her family. Shelby was a "fallen- away Episcopalian" and didn't care if he was married by a Buddhist or a Shintoist, just so he got married. Consequently, Montez made marriage arrangements in the dark. He and Edwards decided that they would throw in Christian trappings and what they thought was appropriate for an Eastern religion.

They built a raised wooden platform where approximately six people could stand comfortably, and they put a white cloth covering on the top and sides. That would allow the guests to witness the marriage ceremony. "That way," Montez said, "I can see, and give a signal if any drunks cause problems."

Edwards parked Lindstrom and Johnson, the two largest crewmen, at strategic locations to assist in case of trouble. Montez convinced them they had to stay sober until the entire ceremony was over. "Lindstrom, you make sure Johnson doesn't get drunk. I promise both you guys a case of beer if you take care of things and don't get drunk early." He hoped one case was enough to bribe them. Lindstrom and Johnson could inhale a case of beer in less than an hour.

They even hired two musicians—one to play the samisen, the other to accompany with an appropriate instrument. Later, Montez added a woman singer. He loved the high-pitched wail of the singing; it would give the marriage ceremony just the right touch of class.

Edwards was a little miffed because he didn't get to hire any musicians and didn't like the samisen. "That there screeching is worse than a banshee in heat. And that plunking of strings gets me a mite edgy."

They tried to get Kimiko and Jun to attend the wedding, but they refused to even consider it. "Never hoppen. GI marry bad girl."

"What if GI married good girl?" Montez asked. "OK, then?"

With perfect logic, Kimiko answered, "If good GI and good girl, hokay. Get married. Go to States."

Montez decided that it was better that the girls didn't come. Edwards agreed. "Ah don't like that talk of good GI and getting hitched and all that stuff."

"For once, Ed, you've finally said something intelligent. Let's enjoy the fiesta, and then we'll get drunk and get laid."

Luckily there was a lull in bombing missions. The scuttlebutt was that it had to do with the possible beginning of peace talks in Korea.

"Monty, I heard that they are sending home the B-29 groups they sent from the States."

"They may even send us home early. But I wouldn't bank on it."

It gave them plenty of time to finalize the preparations. Finally, the day was here.

They put on their Class-A uniforms and arrived at the restaurant, where the marriage was to take place early in the afternoon. Edwards had to check the bunting, banners and balloons again. They both badly needed a beer. "I'm nervous as a virgin in a whorehouse," Edwards said as he inspected the matted floor. Mariko was nowhere to be seen, and Shelby paced the restaurant like an expectant father.

After they finished their inspection, Edwards remarked, "We're ready, vato. Time to have some fun!"

The guests started to dribble in. Lots of strange faces—some they didn't trust. A couple of guys looked older and acted like officers, sniffing around the place like it was an outhouse. However, there were no bars on their uniforms so Montez relaxed.

One officer did show up. First Lt. Tony Lucas was the copilot on their B-29. Those pilots weren't like most of the other officers. Edwards said, "They acted more like us and some were hell on wheels."

Lt. Lucas stayed for a little while, drank some beer, congratulated Shelby and a flustered

Mariko who came out of hiding to say hello to him. Montez knew Lt. Lucas could get into trouble if the Air Force got onto Shelby and found out that one of the officers attended the wedding, crew member or not.

"Now, that's a good ol' boy," Edwards remarked as the lieutenant gave Mariko a kiss and left. "Too bad he's an officer. Guess pilots have to be."

It was nearing the time for the formal ceremony. The restaurant was full of boisterous GIs and Mariko's friends. Edwards didn't like the comments about Mariko and Shelby made by some soldiers.

"I heard some guys are saying that Mariko was a good lay and some other stuff. They're pretty drunk, but they're not from around here and seem harmless."

Nevertheless, Montez was getting a bad feeling. "We better get Shelby and Mariko out of here as soon after the ceremony as possible. He doesn't need to hear this crap."

Edwards agreed. "I'll tell their buggy ride to pick them up early." He looked around the restaurant, "If I hear anybody say anything bad to them, I'm going to kick the shit out of them."

Montez stared at him. Edwards never got into fights. He was a lover. They agreed to stay close to Shelby and Mariko and stop anybody before they said anything to hurt them.

Mariko looked like a rotund angel in a blue-flowered kimono with a matching blue sash around her waist. She clip-clopped her way toward Montez and Edwards in her new getas, wooden sandals wrapped in blue and white cloth. Her hair was piled high on her head, and her face was powdered white, in sharp contrast with her red-painted lips. Her pug nose was also red, maybe from crying. She cried when sad and when happy—the difference in emotion irrelevant.

She greeted them with a low bow. "Arigato gozaimas, arigato gozaimas...you honor me velly much." With another bow, she turned to greet some of her gaily dressed girlfriends who were chattering nonstop in what Montez thought was Japanese or their Luchuan dialect.

Montez, Edwards and their volunteer ground crew members started trying to quiet the noisy crowd. Edwards shushed the group around him. Finally, a small, dignified, brown-coated monk and his assistant slowly walked through the door. The noise level diminished as soon as the servicemen saw the monk. Montez looked about him from his perch on the raised altar. A garden scene unfolded before him: a field of khaki brown surrounding the vivid, multi-hued center of blue, green, red and purple girls' kimonos, headdresses, and white stocking feet in cloth-covered getas. Miraculously, the wedding ceremony commenced after everyone got into his or her allotted position. A few minutes into the ceremony, conducted in Japanese, some of the girls in kimonos began to sniffle.

Montez, from his position on the raised platform, saw everything was going according to plan. Edwards prowled the area like a bloodhound searching for 'coons. The ceremony was short, but it seemed to Montez that it lasted over an hour.

The samisen player and her partners did their best with the music, but no one listened. Right after the monk and his assistant left, the noise level rose. The bride and groom took a long time drinking ceremonial sake and accepting congratulations.

Edwards tried to hustle them toward the door. "Come on, Shelby, yore ride is awaiting. Hell, boy, you can do all that sake drinking in the buggy."

As soon as the couple finished with some ceremonial sake, Montez was finally able to push them out of the restaurant. He walked them to a small grove of dwarf pine, a short distance from the restaurant, for wedding photographs.

Edwards looked like he was ready to cry. "I'll stay behind to make sure there's no trouble."

After a few minutes, he caught up to Montez scowling ferociously. "There's a bunch of drunken dogfaces by the door making cracks. We better get Mariko and Shelby into the cab before those pendejos come out here."

Edwards ran back to the restaurant, Montez grabbed Shelby's arm and pushed him into the cab, Mariko reluctantly following. He threw some rice at them yelling, "You will be sorry," and bellowed to the cab driver to take off. The cab pulled out slowly, too slow for Montez, with Mariko's girl friends chasing it, crying and yelling goodbyes. He looked around and everything appeared to be in order, but a small voice told him it was too good to be true.

The girls returned from seeing Mariko off, and Edwards, being a Southern gentleman, put his arms around two of the prettiest ones and consoled them. "There now, your friend Ed is going to take care of things, so don't you cry."

Then it was time to have some fun. They sat by themselves for a while, congratulating each other. "Well, Ed nothing went wrong, and I can really say I did a hell of a job."

Edwards adjusted his long legs under the small table. "Damned wetbacks," he muttered. "Give them an inch, they take a mile."

They decided to get the music going. "Ed, we better turn on some of your low brow music."

Country music soon filled the air. Rebel yells and Mexican gritos were soon heard. It wasn't long before some inebriated GIs drifted over, irate because Edwards had the prettiest girls. These were the same guys who had been making derogatory comments about Shelby and Mariko.

"Hey, you guys are monopolizing the girls."

Edwards stood up. "You dogfaces have no manners. Cain't you see these here gals need gentlemen and the Army don't have any."

Montez was flabbergasted. Edwards never looked for a fight. One dogface took a swing at Edwards, but missed his mark. He was too drunk.

"You dumb shit," Montez yelled at Edwards. "Now you did it." He turned and hit one soldier flat on the nose and felt something give. Damn! Montez thought. We're in trouble now!

Something hit Montez hard on his shoulder and he couldn't lift his arm. My God, he thought...I'm paralyzed! Then everything happened at once. Bodies hit him from all sides.

He looked for Edwards. His buddy's nose was bleeding but he had a determined look on his face. Desperately Montez held on to someone's head as he pushed his way towards Edwards.

Someone hit him on the head from behind. He let go of the head and from out of nowhere, a fist smashed his temple.

"Ed, some bastard just bashed me...can't move anything!" He couldn't see for the blood, but he got one good lick in on someone before he started to feel dizzy and see strange lights. He felt someone dragging him and tried to stop him. It was Edwards.

"Can't you stand up?" Edwards kept pulling Montez towards the entrance. "Monty, get your ass off the floor and let's get out of here!"

They crawled out the door and limped to a restaurant down the road for a beer. The Mamasan knew them and would take care of them.

Montez was feeling better. Adrenaline coursed through his body. "Shouldn't we go back and see what's happening?"

"Son, you need a keeper. It's lucky that big dogface didn't kill you. I think you broke his nose. Man, he wanted to tear your leg off. Besides, the APs ought to be here soon, so keep out of sight and let's drink our beer."

Montez studied Edwards. He was bloody but had a big grin on his face. "You know, I didn't get to dance to that there bolery music of yours, but I got off one pinche grito." It was the best Spanish Edwards had ever uttered.

When they heard sirens, they knew it was all over. The APs came with a paddy wagon, filled it up with belligerent GIs, and left in short order. Montez started feeling the pain. His shoulder and wrist hurt, and he had a bad headache. Edwards had blood all over the front of his shirt and pants, except where his tie covered his khaki shirt.

Montez laughed at him, "Ed, you look a mess. Someone sure worked you over!"

"Mamasan, bring me a mirror, dozo?" Edwards was handed a long-handled mirror.

"Take a look at that." Montez volunteered. "But at least the blood covers up some of your ugly. Let's get some kimonos from Mamasan and have her wash our clothes."

Edwards handed the mirror to Montez, who peered into it. His face and the front of his torn khaki blouse and trousers were crimson with blood. "I think I'm bleeding to death!"

Edwards was busy negotiating with Mamasan about the laundry.

"I need a medic! I need a beer!" Montez yelled. "Some buddy he is. Here I am bleeding to death and he's talking."

After a few minutes, Mamasan told them to be still and closed their various wounds with tape and washed the blood away.

"You joto san, GI. You numbah one. Never fight. Why you fight now? Drink mizu, more betta than biru."

"Mamasan, we need biru now, not water." Montez pleaded, "Biru good for GI. Make him strong again."

Mamasan made some clucking noises but in the end she gave in. Bandaged and spent, they contentedly sat back on some hideously colored cushions, sipped their beer, and started to recount what happened to them. With each beer, the stories got better. With a little time, they could write a movie script.

Montez cautiously felt his swollen, cut lips and checked for loose teeth. "That was the best-damned wedding I have ever been to, but I never want another even close to it."

Edwards gingerly touched his swollen lips. "Amen to that, brother. Amen to that."

Chapter 7

Another Misfit

Montez dressed in oily, torn fatigue pants, walked out of the cool, air-conditioned Operations shack, juggling five cokes for his crew and ran smack-dab into a general, spilling some soda on the general's smartly creased khaki shirt.

He stared in disbelief. It was General Douglas MacArthur. Montez admired MacArthur more than Eisenhower or even George Patton, and the thought of soiling the general's crisp, natty uniform with soda and grease from his unworthy body numbed him. Christ, he wanted to fall on his sword.

The General looked good in his uniform, with that erect body and craggy face. He stared at Montez for a moment as if he were an amoeba under a microscope. Montez was ready to give his name, rank, and serial number so the APs could throw him in the guardhouse. But the general just strode past, ignoring Montez and his entreaties for forgiveness.

Scurrying out of the shack balancing the offending cokes, Montez turned to see if the General was still there. Watching him with a bemused, distant smile was Sergeant Solomon, the operations clerk.

❖❖❖❖❖

Returning to his ship, Montez passed MacArthur's private aircraft, a C-121 Transport, named "Bataan."

"Hey, you guys!" Montez yelled when he reached his aircraft. "I just bumped into General MacArthur! I spilled Coke all over his uniform!" That would be enough for now—he would elaborate on his story a little later.

Airman 2nd Class Lindstrom snorted, "Christ, you can't let Montez out of sight. He always comes back with some screwy story to tell."

Montez and the rest of the crew were jealous of Lindstrom. The sun deeply tanned the tall, blond, blue-eyed ground crewman's skin mahogany, turned his hair almost white, and made his eyes even bluer. Women couldn't keep their hands off of him. He went out with hard-to-get American women in the Red Cross, WAFS and other officer material. When he came back from his innumerable dates, the crew pumped him for every delectable morsel of information he would deign to give.

"Lindstrom, you dumb Swede," Montez

replied, "You wouldn't know the truth if it hit your hard, empty head."

"The General wouldn't let a grease ball like you even get close to him," replied Lindstrom. "Now me, I'm an all-American boy. The General would ask me over for a beer and advice on the war."

Lindstrom was a good-natured guy with a ready smile, but Montez had to insure that his tale was believed as Gospel before he stretched it. "Look, you dummy, I can take you over to his plane. The guard saw what happened," Montez said, with just the right level of indignation. Of course, he didn't see a guard near the General's plane; and anyway, no one would check his story.

Staff Sergeant Easley, the assistant crew chief from Mississippi, broke in with, "Yew boys quit yore funnin' and git to work."

"OK, Sarge," Lindstrom and Montez replied and pretended to start working diligently.

Sergeant Easley was a not-too-bright man in his late thirties with a beer belly which he tried to minimize unsuccessfully by wearing tight fatigue coveralls. His efforts only made him look like a large waddling penguin. Montez couldn't understand how the man graduated from Aircraft and Engine Mechanics School. The sergeant could hardly read above the fifth-grade level, so how could he have understood the math and complex aerodynamics taught in the school? However, he bragged about how he knew a couple of good ol' boys that were instructors at the A&E school. On the other hand, he was not a person you wanted to be friends with; he smiled a cruel smile easily and couldn't say five words without derogatory namecalling. They all cussed and learned as many swear words as they could. However, Sergeant Easley's deeply felt swearing and hatred of Negroes and those he considered foreigners, were disconcerting to the ground crew. Montez felt uneasy when Sergeant Easley, in his singular, ingratiating manner, talked to him. He discovered that the ground crew felt the same way and even walked the other way when they saw him coming.

Sergeant Easley saw Edwards and Montez talking earnestly while attaching the cowling over the engine frame. With his easy smile under washed-out blue eyes he said, "Hey, Montez, when ya goin' to join the greaser air force? They need some good men."

"At least they'd hire me, Sarge. You wouldn't have a chance." Montez was careful not to go too heavy on his reply. Easley would retaliate and have him pull extra guard duty.

The ground crew started to work on their assigned duties so that Easley wouldn't bother them. They never asked him questions regarding the aircraft, The Pesky Fly. He was technically incompetent as an assistant crew chief, and they relied on their crew chief, Technical Sergeant Pappas. Sergeant Pappas used Easley as an aircraft babysitter; Easley was always at work on time, the last to leave, and faithful to Pappas.

Waiting for the 6X6 truck for a ride to the mess hall, Montez watched most of the men stick a cigarette in their mouths and light it — the tips burned red as they sucked, the smoke curling into their tearing, blinking eyes while the searing heat of the sun beat on their sunburned bodies. He again wondered why they like to smoke those hot tubes in the searing sun.

"Look at that big goddamned rat in the wheel well!" Sergeant Moretti yelled.

The airmen turned to the front wheel well of the B-29 and gaped at a huge rat sitting on the flight log lying on the strut above the tire.

"Cheerist! It looks like he's reading the flight log," Edwards said. "Maybe he wants to know where they're going tomorrow."

Some of the men ran to shack next to the aircraft hardstand and picked up shovels, a hoe and large sticks. One grabbed his carbine and started for the rat. "Put that weapon down, you idiot," someone yelled. "You want to kill somebody?"

They all advanced slowly trying to encircle the rat.
"Don't let him jump back into the plane," one of the men warned.

"I'm going to knock him to the ground, so be ready." Montez positioned himself with the largest piece of wood he could find. He kept staring at the rat — his grayish-brown body was about eighteen inches long, the hanging tail the same length, his dark eyes balefully glinted as he watched the airmen creep up to him. The rat didn't move, just watched as if he didn't care — this was his home.

Lindstrom hit the rat hard enough to knock him to the concrete hardstand, and the crew rushed in to kill him. The cornered rat angrily bared chisel-like teeth, his furry sides heaving with fright. The airmen started striking him with whatever they had found until the enraged rat ran toward the edge of the hardstand, straight at Edwards.

Montez had never seen a man jump so high from a standing position. The sergeant with the hoe swung for the rat's head but hit his tail instead, cutting about eight inches off, as the screaming rat went down a hole just off the hardstand. Morretti and Hardy each got a five-gallon can of fuel and poured it into the hole. They threw a match into the hole and flames flared up from the holes connected by tunnels around the hardstand.

Montez heard the rat and whatever else was in the tunnel scream in pain for at least two minutes. "Man, this place could have caught on fire, even blown ourselves up," Montez said. "This was the dumbest thing we ever did."

A crestfallen Moretti and Hardy walked over to the group of men. "We knew nothing would happen to the plane," Hardy explained lamely. "Guess we didn't think about all the holes tying together."

"You idiots!" Edwards yelled, still feeling foolish after his fright. "I hope no one saw this."

Montez knew Edwards would be unhappy when the crew remembered his acrobatics. The strange part of the whole episode was that they knew there must be a rat eating the box lunches. But a monster rat? He had even made up a ditty about the rat and now it had an ending.

"Ed, remember we talked about the rat over a month ago? Well, I wrote a little ditty named the 'Nosy Rat.' Do you want to hear it?" Without waiting for an answer, Montez struck a pose and recited:

>The food was eaten,
>but not by the crew.
>Holes in the boxes,
>yet tied up like new.
>
>It was not me,
>it was not you.
>Must be the rat,
>not the B-29 crew.
>
>We finally found him,
>as huge as a cat,
>reading the plane's log,
>so cocky and fat.
>
>Sadly we killed him,
>burned him in fire.
>Buried him deeply,
>screaming in dire.

"Boy, you just ain't a poet," Edwards said, covering his ears with his grimy hands. "I don't need to hear stuff like that on an empty stomach."

Montez decided to forget his MacArthur story and he better not say anything about the fire. Then he remembered that Sergeant Solomon saw him bump into the General. He'd ask Solomon to tell Edwards about the incident, and Edwards would check out his story. He walked over to the Operations shack and verified that the General's plane was gone. The Nissan hut was cool, bare of furniture or any niceties and empty, except for Sgt. Solomon.

Feeling foolish, Montez said, "I know this thing sounds stupid, but I made a bet that I bumped into General MacArthur here in Operations."

Sol found the whole thing amusing but decided to go along with Montez's story — even embellished it some between puffs from an old stained pipe. "I'll tell them that you spilled Coke all over the General's medals."

"That's great." Montez replied. "I owe you one. You know, I've seen you several times at the library, but nowhere else. Not even the NCO Club."

Rubbing his pipe some, Sergeant Solomon replied, "I just don't go out much. Have no need to — although I go to the movies once in a while. By the way, call me Sol. Everyone else does."

Montez had a million questions but held

back because he thought he'd already asked too many questions. Sol was of average height and weight with dark brown hair and watchful brown eyes — an average looking man in everyway. It was his controlled, alert demeanor that caught Montez's attention. Although he appeared to be a reticent, distant individual, he was friendly enough when approached, Montez thought. Despite that aloof bearing, Sol had a droll look to him that perked Montez's interest.

That opened their conversation into books that they had read, where they were from, and their dislike of military life. The two sergeants ended their conversation when an officer came in the back door. They departed with a vague promise to see each other at the library.

Montez soon forgot about the conversation when he didn't have to prove anything to the crew; everybody heard about General MacArthur stopping in Okinawa. His buddies didn't want to hear about his bumping into MacArthur — it seemed he was Montez's hero only.

Montez complained to Edwards, "You know we work with cretins who can't see that MacArthur will go down in history as one of our greatest Generals."

Edwards didn't care either, "Hell, boy, don't you know ol' 'Dugout Doug' left his troops behind while he went to Australia."

"My God!" Montez exclaimed. "You can't believe that old canard. Even you should know better. Don't you have schools in those hills where you come from?"

"Shoot, boy," Edwards replied. "My grammar school graduated smarter people than all those fruity Californy schools."

They argued that piece of history until it was chewed up pretty well. Montez never did get anyone to appreciate his brush with history, no matter how he embellished the story.

❖❖❖❖❖

The base library, about as complete as the ones in those little dusty towns where Montez lived, made him feel comfortable. It had that remembered musty book smell and the same quiet feel. A deeper reason was the feeling he was a burden at home and barely tolerated by his stepmother. The library was his real home, always welcoming him with open arms no matter how rebellious and inconsiderate he was. Montez remembered his friends asking why he liked going to the library so much. He couldn't adequately explain it without sounding priggish. He didn't have to explain it to Edwards or Shelby.

Two weeks after Montez talked to Sol, they met going into the library. Montez saw that Sol was surprised to see him at the library especially with two history books under his arm. He guessed that it didn't fit into the boozing and chasing women picture Sol probably had of airmen.

"Notice you like history," said Sol.

"Well, I'm into Greek history and mythology again," answered Montez. "I've read about everything I can get my hands on at this place. I'll start on something else soon — I'm pretty tired of it. Guess I just get hooked and read about a subject until I drop."

They turned in their books and started to discuss history and literature. They discussed their common birthplace, California, and their background.

"I'm an agnostic, but a cultural Roman Catholic — I feel like I'm Catholic," Montez said.

"And I'm a cultural Jew, but I know I'm a Jew."

The only Jews that Montez had known or rather seen, were old men in black with long beards sitting by windows in East Los Angeles where he stayed for a short period time when he was very young. Sol also lived in the same neighborhood, Boyle Heights, a few years before Montez. Sol explained it was a Jewish community but they gradually moved to West Los Angeles and the San Fernando Valley. It was strange, thought Montez, that two dissimilar people from the same neighborhood would meet in Okinawa during a war.

Sol, to Montez surprise, had a Bachelor's degree in English and a Master's degree in English literature. Sol was an enigma. What's a guy with a master's degree doing in the Air Force as an enlisted man? Montez could understand Shelby with the problems he had, but not Sol. He had no problems that he could see and, anyway, he was around six years older than most of us, had a degree, and should know how to handle himself. Montez figured he would ask him a little bit more the next time he saw him.

A short time after Montez discovered Sol was Jewish, he found Edwards reading yet another book on the philosopher Spinoza. Edwards was in his Spinoza mood and would read everything on him until he collapsed.

"Ed," Montez asked. "Did you know Sol is Jewish? By the way, did you know Spinoza was a Jew?"

"Is that right?" he replied. "I never talked to a Jew. I never even met one. Do they look different? I know Spinoza gave up being a Jew."

"You idiot," Montez replied. "You know Sol. He has a masters degree in lit and he's not an officer. Think of that. And yes, I know Spinoza gave up being a Jew, but he didn't become a Christian."

Edwards told Montez what he thought about Sol's advanced education and low lifestyle as an enlisted man. "Maybe that boy's not too swift and couldn't be an officer." He added, "Just because he has a master's degree doesn't make him a genius. Look at Captain Phillips—that boy's dumb as the wall and he graduated from Yale."

The next time Montez saw Sol was when he and Airman 2nd class Morelli, walked into the Operations shack for Cokes. They found Sergeant

Easley loudly complaining to a fellow assistant crew chief, "Yew knows how all them Negroes are. And thar now gonna to be with white folk in the barracks. This here Air Force is full of them and thar Jew boy friends too. Yawl mark ma words."

Montez darted a look toward Sol. He didn't blink an eye. That same quiet, watchful look never left his face, although he seemed to suck on his ever-present pipe a little harder. Montez then glanced at Sergeant Easley to see if he was goading Sol. He wasn't even aware that Sol was there and probably didn't know that Sol was Jewish. Easley never commented on it, and Montez figured that he would have if he knew. The two staff sergeants walked out of the building, still discussing the demise of the U.S. Air Force.

Montez went over to Sol. "Do you ever get pissed off when you hear stuff like that? I have to decide if I should say something when some bastard calls me or someone else a wetback, greaser, or some other endearment."

Sol ruminated for awhile, sucking on his pipe, and finally said, "John, I usually think about it, too, before I say anything. I consider the person, the circumstances, and whether it's useful to answer. Now that Easley is too stupid. He wouldn't understand, or care, what I said."

"You know, "Montez replied, "I would like to talk to you sometime about situations like that and how you handle them. Most of my Mexican-American friends tend to get a little aggravated and end up in a fight. There must be a better way. I am a lover in training, not a fighter." Montez left it at that. Strange...Sol was the only person who called him by his first name.

Morelli joined them with the Cokes and said, "Hey, Paisans. I walked way over here and didn't see General MacArthur."

"Christ almighty, Morelli, MacArthur left days ago."

When they returned to their plane, they found Army or Marine grunts — it was hard to tell — running in full combat gear in the bush around their plane and the flight line. They scrambled up the wing joining Edwards to get a good view of this theatre.

Montez yelled, "It looks like they're practicing assault tactics in the bush...maybe to attack a North Korean airbase."

They started to hoot and holler at the grunts. They figured the filthy troops couldn't do anything to them or even say anything because they had their officers looking.

"Boy, I nearly joined those Marines," Montez remarked as they watched them run and fall and generally do things that the human body is not suited for. "Just look at them mucking around in that slop. I thank Allah, Jove and every other deity in the pantheon for keeping me from joining that select group of men — as they like to say."

"Hey, they look like they're having fun." Edwards answered, as he postured and yelled at the troops. "I should've joined the infantry and been a dang hero."

After the fun was over, they went back to work. Edwards asked Montez, "What are you going to do tonight? I have goddamned guard duty tonight." Montez knew Shelby was with his wife, and he didn't want to disturb them.

"I don't know, maybe go to the library."

Edwards didn't mind guarding the aircraft all night. Montez did, especially when you had to go through the inside of the plane every hour. It was spooky going through there with every sharp object catching your fatigues as you worked your way to the front of the plane and out the hatch. It felt like hands of the dead were grabbing you, trying to keep you in that black coffin. Montez hated it when a part of his clothes hooked on to some piece of metal. He would quickly turn around, heart pumping and shine his flashlight beam in that direction, then feel foolish and go on with the inspection. Once outside, Montez would stare at a moon, so large and bright that he felt he could grab it, if his arms were just a little longer. After staring at the immense yellow Okinawan moon for a couple of hours, Montez felt like howling like a wolf, and sometimes did. He didn't know if others guarding their planes got into the howling mood. He knew, however, that he heard long wolf-like howls from far off in the night.

Montez found Sol, his ever-present, unlighted pipe in hand, deep in some sort of historical research. Not disturbing him, Montez went to the stacks to sample books at random.

An hour later, Sol came over to say hello, remarking, "John, I only see you at the library or on the flight line. Otherwise you seem to disappear."

"Well, to tell you the truth," Montez replied, "Ed and I get off the base every minute we can. We also have different hours from most guys because of our plane. You never know what's going to happen on a mission, you know, or what kind of work we're going to do on it."

As an afterthought, Montez commented, "I never see you at the village or anywhere else on the base." Montez nearly added that he'd never seen him with anyone, anywhere.

"I've been to several villages but not much doing there. Actually, I guess I'm somewhat of a loner. It's not that much fun going to town by yourself."

Montez stared at him. Not much to do there! He can't be that old, maybe he's about twenty-six, at the oldest twenty-eight.

"Why don't you go with us?" Montez invited. "We always find some interesting things to do...and I can introduce you to Shelby. He's a buddy of mine who married an Okinawan girl and lives in the village most of the time."

Montez could see that his interest was aroused, especially when he mentioned Shelby and his situation. Unlike Shelby, however, Sol just thanked him but didn't follow through on a meeting. They continued talking outside the library for a couple of hours enjoying the remnants of the dark orange-going-purple sky. "I wish I could capture in words the colors above those mountains," Sol added. "Maybe one of these days I will. I'm the most prolific, unpublished writer in the US; but like you and a quest for a college degree, I'll persevere."

Under that aloof, unemotional exterior, Montez found a humorous, even witty man. After a while, Montez was laughing loudly and openly — something he hardly ever did. He didn't appreciate most humor; in fact, Montez dreaded the ubiquitous "Did you hear this one" joke. Sol didn't tell jokes. Sol somehow threaded humorous comments and stories into the conversation. His stories had different meanings or double entendres. Montez could hardly wait to have Edwards and his droll humor meet with Sol's quick-witted repartee.

Montez found in Sol a person who did not make friends easily. Sol was reticent and reserved, giving the impression of a snob or recluse. Once you pierced that shell, he lost that taciturn response and became animated. Montez also felt that Sol's shell shielded him not only from Gentiles, but also Jews — perhaps Montez understood that because he had his own shell against the world. At any rate, both were soon kibitzing and a friendship had started. By God, he thought, I now have three real friends, and all within a short period of time. How strange that it took over one year to find one true friend and now three!

Edwards and Sol finally got together about a month after the library meeting. Edwards wasn't too keen on getting together with Sol. He really didn't want him in the group. Sol was older, very educated, didn't chase women, and horrors, didn't drink much beer.

He just didn't fit in, or as Edwards elegantly put it, "That boy just got too much class for us'n. He belongs with them there officers and their snooty white women they have carnal knowledge with."

"Christ sakes, Ed," Montez interjected, "You are getting snooty yourself. You're just jealous because you can't get your grimy paws on their women."

Preening himself like a rooster, Edwards replied, "Ah don't want to talk 'bout this 'cause I'm a gent and gents don't talk 'bout ladies. But boy, you have wounded me deeply, so I have to tell you 'bout my fling with this Red Cross gal...."

"Forget it Ed, I think I see Sol coming in."

While Sol was threading his way through the tables in the NCO Club, Montez thought of ways to get these characters to at least be friendly with each other. There was no need. Sol was fascinated with Edwards and his use of the Queen's English. He loved Edwards' country sayings and stories and, in return, Edwards was enthralled with Sol's Jewish anecdotes and his ripping turn of an English phrase.

"This boy knows how to say things with dashing elegance," Edwards would exclaim at some well-turned phrase. "We call it panache in the Tennessee hills."

"It's not pronounced pana chey," Montez corrected and quickly changed the subject. "Where did you get your degree?" he asked of Sol.

"UCLA," replied Sol. "Seems I've been in school all of my life."

"You're lucky," replied Montez, "I wish.... "

"John, you can do anything you want. You've already read more about religion, philosophy and history than most college grads."

"I don't even have a real high school diploma," replied Montez. "I've finished all the USAFI courses needed for a high school diploma and taken all the classes to get into one of the California colleges when I get out." Then nodding towards Edwards, "Even this fool has a high school diploma."

"Well, I'd take umbrage at that remark," replied Edwards. "But, ah know that my poor uneducable friend here is mightily jealous of me and other educated folks. I have tried to educate him, but he jus' cain't get it."

Montez rolled his eyes. He should have known not to bring up his lack of a high school diploma in front of Edwards.

"Gentlemen, gentlemen, we are getting off the subject here. We need not tarry in this ill-favored abode when yon village is a relatively short distance away."

Edwards and Montez looked at each other.

"Y'all mean you want to go to those dens of iniquity?" Edwards asked, followed by Montez, "You know that those places we go to are full of women and booze...."

"Look, you misguided misanthropes, I like women as well as the next man." Sol added, "Just because I have shown a modicum of gentility and grace does not mean I will not lay siege to a woman's virtue. It would do you well to pay attention to my savoir-faire, to my comity — you ill-mannered louts."

The two young airmen looked at each other, and Edwards said, "Well, it looks like we have another neophyte to train."

Montez sighed, "Ed, I start worrying when you use words like 'neophyte.' I better take over and keep Sol from harm by those nasty women."

Edwards put a protective arm around Sol's shoulder. "Ah think he's also loaded with money, not as much as Shelby, but 'nough to keep us happy while he's in training."

"Machiavelli wrote," said Montez, "'He should learn from the fox and the lion...one has to be a fox to recognize traps, and a lion to frighten off wolves.' Unfortunately, I think we're the wolves."

Chapter 8

Rest and Recuperation

Airmen rarely paid attention to admonitions on the bulletin board: *Use condoms to avoid venereal disease. If you had unprotected contact with the indigenous populace, use a prophylactic kit and get a penicillin injection upon return to base.*

Montez, however, was due for R & R and checked the board daily.

Finally, a list pinned to the crumbling cork bulletin board showed that he and half his crew were scheduled for eleven days in Hong Kong, the Philippines or Japan. Montez preferred Hong Kong, but his crew voted for Japan. He didn't want to go alone and Edwards was not on the list. However, it was a good time to go. Shelby and Mariko were honeymooning, and Sol was busy with work postponed due to his village trips. Montez had prepared for his trip by stockpiling cartons of cigarettes from the PX. The old timers told him they were worth their weight in gold in Japan.

When the day arrived, Montez dragged a large faded-green duffle bag full of cigarettes and a small bundle of clothes aboard the C-54. He figured he could always wash clothes and used almost all of the space for his treasure. The rest of the passengers had the same idea, as they struggled into the aircraft with their heavy loads of booty. It was illegal, but what were the authorities going to do — throw them all in the guardhouse?

The C-54 touched down in Tachikawa Air Force Base at noon. The military personnel on board vibrated with anticipation. Montez's painfully saved one-hundred dollars was pooled with crew members to rent a Geisha house in the small town of Kunitachi, a few miles from Tokyo. It belonged to them, complete with Geisha girls, for ten days.

Montez spent most of the time on the immaculate grounds surrounding the Geisha house. The light-brown wood and paper structure was hidden from prying eyes by an enclosing ten-foot wall. Leaves from knurled pine trees dappled the well-kept tall grass. Twisted bonsai trees, harmoniously placed, graced the open area surrounding the seven-bedroom resort. A clear stream meandered through the garden, under an ornately carved red bridge and around the house. Young girls in blue, green and silver-white kimonos glided silently through the tea-house, taking care of their awed guests.

"Hey, Monty, I bet all the rich Japanese lived

like this before the big war," Morelli said, as he admired the garden and the pretty girls. "I can't believe the Japanese would start a war with all this at home."

Montez nodded agreement; however, he felt that everything was too perfect—everything, every blade of grass was in its place. People who created this fairyland could believe they could make the world in their image, whether the world wanted to or not.

Once the men became bored with perfection, forays to Tokyo became more common. Montez and his crew boarded the bullet train, looking like well-fed giants in a car full of small, slim people and twenty minutes later be in Tokyo. The Japanese passengers looked at them surreptitiously, not with fear, but with curiosity. These country people were not used to tall, hairy Americans.

He'd heard the Japanese disliked the smell of the meat-eating Americans. He unconsciously moved away from an old wrinkled man standing close to him, then recognized his action and smiled inwardly. He missed Edwards and his corny comments. He would've had some good stuff to say. The company he teamed up with was Al, a quiet crew member of another aircraft at loose ends, since his buddy wasn't on this trip. Before his trip to the city, Montez sold at least twenty cartons of cigarettes to a Japanese groundskeeper at the teahouse and several more to pay for all the beer and sake he could drink.

Tokyo, with its bright, garish lights and crowded streets, was full of obviously poor people wearing worn, faded cotton shirts and nondescript trousers; although many of the younger women were wearing modern western clothes and the men were in dark suits. Kimonos and high wooden clogs still graced the street — thank God. Soldiers and sailors of all nationalities walked among the throng of people, Americans making up the majority of the foreigners. Montez found the Japanese people to be in a hurry — polite, unlike other Asian people he met.

The department stores were full of soldiers buying every knick-knack in sight. He tried to buy some lacquer-ware with cigarettes, but the store clerk refused. Montez turned to leave; two young Japanese men stopped him, each one offering to take the cigarettes off his hand for a good price.

"One dolla fifty for one carton," offered the more aggressive man.

"Two dolla for one carton," said the other man. "That top dollah."

"Okay. You got a deal if you buy all of them." Montez opened a cheap satchel with twelve cartons of cigarettes for viewing. The young man took out a large roll of script held together by a rubber band and pulled out twenty-four dollars. The roll wasn't reduced a fraction. Montez felt like a rich man knowing he would even have money left over for some Okinawan action.

On his second visit to Tokyo, Montez found

an immense dance hall: two huge floors with two bands playing, one on each side of a walled, revolving platform—they alternated playing rumbas, tangos, and American popular music. Montez saw at least a hundred beautiful dance girls waiting demurely for someone to ask them to dance. He was told they weren't prostitutes but were paid to dance. Most of the customers were United Nations soldiers and sailors; a few Japanese men sat with the girls. Even in the well-ventilated dancehall, he smelled the perfumed fragrance of the girls, a scent rare in Okinawa.

"Harris, do you see that vision in the long white dress: She's the most beautiful thing I've seen in months," sighed Montez. He quickly walked over to her table and asked her to dance in Japanese. He figured he had to use every advantage he could dream up to convince her to go out with him. It worked. She was impressed to find an American GI who could speak Japanese, or at least try. After several dances and earnest pleading, she agreed to go on a date.

Michiko had a beautiful smile, cat-like eyes and a faint scent of gardenias. He was smitten. Montez found a little round table with a droopy white flower in a vase on the outskirt of the hall and danced until she tired. He reluctantly let her go home not quite believing that she would keep their date tomorrow.

Michiko showed up at the ice cream parlor at exactly the time agreed upon—he was there half hour early. They spent the following seven days at the Kabuki Theater; at Japanese movies where she cried over everything; and visited parks and temples, holding hands, learning all about her. The days were a blur of colors and emotion—they met early and suddenly it was night. He saw others, Westerners, with Japanese women and wondered if they were in love or just "short timers."

He didn't want to be like the "short timers" so they went to small villages, far from Tokyo, to eat and walk and talk. They understood each other perfectly by adding gestures, stroking and smiling at their attempts at each other's language.

She asked him in broken English, "You tell about home town and Papa-san and Mama-san? You have girlfriend? You have tocusan money?"

He smiled and told her, in English and broken Japanese, "Oh, I'm just a little rich." Why destroy an image. He also had her sell the rest of his cigarettes through her friends and bought her a beautiful and expensive hair comb.

He knew they only had a few days together—that he shouldn't get too close to Michiko. His reserve broke one night, "Michiko, I don't think I can leave you. I want to be here with you."

"You no can stay." She held his hand. "Ano ne. Please, listen. You go stockade. I love you. Wakarimaska? You understand? You my steky boy—not go stockade."

Montez smiled when she called him her "steky" boy. He called her his "steky" girl or "nice" in Japanese. Nevertheless, he couldn't stop seeing her and threw caution to the wind. He was going to stay with her until they found him.

It ended unexpectedly; her mother, who lived in a small village far from Tokyo, was very ill and Michiko wanted to be with her. Montez was disconsolate; he'd be gone long before she returned.

The following day, at the train station, they promised never to forget each other — to write every day. Both knew the brief interlude was over as she kissed him goodbye and got into the train. He thought his heart would break as he watched the train quickly move out of the station.

Two days before his scheduled return to Okinawa, while walking dejectedly on the side streets off the Ginza, Montez found himself looking at the largest beer hall he had ever seen. The familiar smell of beer and tobacco smoke permeated the air as he entered. He counted twenty three, foot-square, weight-bearing columns with shiny blue-green tiles holding up a high ceiling. There were hundreds of soldiers from every country representing the United Nations. A couple pitchers of beer later, Montez answered a talkative, large-mustached Australian soldier, sporting a bush hat.

"What's the matter, mate?" asked the ebullient Aussie. "Looks like you lost your best friend. Hey, Tommy, bring your mates over here." He bellowed to a New Zealand soldier, who moved over to their heavy, dark-wood table, wet with beer. He was followed by a Canadian and a South African soldier, each with a pitcher of beer.

"The Yank appears to be having the blues. What you say we cheer him up?"

"Maybe he got a 'dear john' letter," the Kiwi replied. "I got one 'bout three months ago. Best thing that ever happened to me. I was balmy, going to splice up with that one — well, that's another story."

The friendliness of the group and another pitcher of beer did cheer up Montez. He had never met such outgoing people. They made Edwards seem like a bashful bumpkin. After a few more pitchers of beer, the Aussie and the Canadian decided to get together a group representing the UN, they called some more soldiers to join them — an Indian Gurkha, a Greek, and two Turks… they came in a pair. Montez hoped they wouldn't invite any more. Sixteen countries sent troops to Korea. A couple of British soldiers invited themselves; and after some more pitchers of beer, a Colombian soldier joined them at the three hastily combined tables.

Montez didn't know whose bright idea it was to become blood brothers, but the now drunk soldiers agreed — as a gesture of brotherhood. One of the Turks pulled out a huge knife and cut his lower arm, then gestured with his bleeding arm for all the soldiers to do the same — which they happily did.

Blood mingled freely with the spilt beer on the three tables. It looked like a slaughterhouse. Someone passed the knife to Montez. With reluctance, he sliced his arm, but the knife was razor sharp and he cut too deeply. Blood flowed. Montez, certain he had cut an artery, knew he was going to bleed to death. The Turks looked on approvingly. The last thing he remembered was chug-a-lugging a pitcher of beer with his Aussie friend and discussing the fate of the soldiers at the table. They were all infantry and would be back on the front lines in a few days. Montez felt terrible that he wasn't going to fight and volunteered to go with them.

Montez didn't die, but he wished he had when he woke up the next morning in a strange barrack. Rays of bright light cut into his eyes and aching head. Realizing he was only in his shorts, he frantically looked for his uniform. Christ, he'd been shanghaied, he thought. Anything can happen in the Orient. He felt pain coming from his arm and saw a large bandage covering his lower arm and hand. Montez touched the bandage gingerly, and then he remembered the Turks and that sharp knife. Jesus Cheerist!

A body in the next bunk moaned; a tousled brown head of hair slowly appeared from under the blanket. A vaguely familiar face with a huge brown mustache, smiled at him.

"How you feel Yank?" said the mustache,

kicking a brown blanket off hairy, white legs and feet enclosed in ratty-looking brown socks.

"I don't feel too good. Where in the hell am I? Where's my uniform?" Montez asked, getting to a sitting position but not moving his aching head any further.

"Take it easy, mate. Don't you remember? You're going with us to our camp in Korea—you bloody well insisted."

"To Korea—what the hell you talking about? Where am I?"

"You're lucky, mate," said the Australian with a wolfish grin. "You didn't go with the Turks. They're rough cobs. Like to sneak into enemy lines with those bloody knives of theirs and cut gook throats. They're the only soldiers the gooks are afraid of. Anyway, I saved your sorry ass and brought you safely home, as it is." He waved his arm. "My name's Bob Ahearn—they call me Rooster." He pulled out a stubby cigar, which had seen better days and pushed it into his mouth. "You're in an Aussie camp near Tokyo. Mamasan will have your uniform ready in a couple of hours."

Montez let out a sigh of relief. "How do I get back to Tokyo—or better yet, to Kunitachi?"

"First thing first, mate. Let's get some food down us, and then I'll show you around. You can wear one of my uniforms till yours is ready."

"Hell, I can't do that. I'll get arrested by your military police for being out of uniform. And besides, I got a hangover that won't quit. I can't go anywhere."

"The military police, as you call the buggers, don't fool with us much. I return to Korea in a couple of days." Rooster bared his teeth in what he must have thought passed for a smile. If you still want to go with us, they'll welcome any warm body on the front lines."

Montez decided Rooster was brain-damaged at birth but a nice enough guy. Nevertheless, he put on the baggy, scratchy Aussie trousers. He added a maroon beret, though he couldn't swear to the color. Montez imagined he looked okay until he looked in a mirror: blood-shot eyes, dark circles, pale sweaty skin, and an ugly stubble of a beard. He was taken to the Aussie mess hall for breakfast, where he was offered bean, bread and sausages; he couldn't see anything else edible except for a huge pot of grey lumpy oatmeal and blessed coffee and tea.

"If you like this, we get the same stuff for lunch and dinner," offered Rooster. "Except they trade that delicious oatmeal for mashed 'taters and add some green stuff. We always have beans, though."

The food went down without incident; Montez sat quietly, not wanting to disturb the lump in his stomach. Finally, Rooster convinced him he'd live, and he should see the camp. Even though Montez was afraid that the officers might question him, he enjoyed himself and had tea with milk and sugar — a first for him — at the canteen on wheels. He met several Aussies and all were friendly, amusing and a little crazy. But it fit them.

The camp was like any military installation: brown, green, and tan colors; dark green-grey trucks and equipment, mostly American, a shimmering, green-blue lake; gliding ducks and swans that left wakes like contrails. Drooping, large-leafed trees saved the camp from total drabness. Rooster showed him off to all of his buddies, like a captured Panda bear. Montez began to enjoy himself, especially after he drank a bottle of cold beer to chase the hangover away.

Rooster tried to convince him to stay but finally with reluctance gave him his clean uniform. He stopped trying talk Montez into stopping off at his base in Korea. At the bus stop outside the camp, Rooster told him to write. If I don't write back, mate, the little buggers got me."

The two remaining days in Japan passed like a perfumed dream. Montez spent time in the secluded garden drinking in the quiet, thinking of Michiko. Was she thinking of him? He admired the oddly shaped bonsai trees and the large gold and red koi in the pond.

While his crew was in Tokyo, several girls with nothing better to do bathed him twice a day in a large, wooden tub full of extremely hot water. After several inquiries regarding his depression, he told them of his affection for Michiko.

"My goodness, this velly, velly sad," commiserated one of the hostesses, while the others clicked their tongues. "Your heart heavy, ne? I cry for you."

The rest of the girls nodded their head in agreement. Later, his three favorites fed him small pieces of pork meat and vegetable sizzling over a hibachi, using ivory chopsticks. In the evenings, when the crew returned from their sightseeing, they couldn't understand why all the Geisha girls favored Montez, at their expense.

The return flight to Okinawa was quiet and restful. Montez and his crew were deep in their memories, putting off the inevitable return to duty. Montez felt he had changed somehow but didn't know how. He spent some time making up a terrific story for Edwards: he was attacked by some thugs, but his martial arts training saved him, except for a deep cut on his arm.

Chapter 9

Our Home

At times, thought Montez, the days and weeks would crawl, but the last few weeks had passed quickly. Shelby and Mariko bought a little brown clapboard house with a red-tiled roof. It wasn't much, but it had what they wanted including a large refrigerator for Montez and Edwards' beer. Local workmen renovated the two bedroom house: new paper and wood sliding doors, refinished hardwood floors in the front room and kitchen, and painted window sills — red to match the roof. The newly-weds bought the largest and costliest bedroll any of them had ever seen and installed new reed tatami mats. All in all, this was an expensive renovation, but Shelby didn't have to worry about money.

The cottage, as Shelby called it, was nestled near large pines trees that partly shadowed the flowering ground cover. The cottage was hidden from the main road that led to the village and was close to the airbase, but not too close. At

first, Montez recalled, the stand-offish Okinawan neighbors wouldn't talk to Shelby or
Mariko. An American airman married to a former Okinawan prostitute, and buying a nice
house in their secluded and quiet neighborhood
offended their sensibilities.

Mariko wanted to move. "I no like it here."
She complained to Montez. "Snooty neighbors
no like Mariko. Me good girl now. Shelbysan no
like it—he velly mad."

Finally, Shelby decided to take action, even
though it might backfire. He took a reluctant
Mariko from neighbor to neighbor and introduced themselves. The surprised neighbors
bowed and reluctantly acknowledged the insis-
tent airman's greetings. The neighbors didn't
come around to borrow sugar, but they started
to nod and smile to the newly married couple
working in the garden—after seeing that the
stigma of a prostitute didn't rub off. Shelby did
not give up. He wanted his child, and he
planned to have one immediately, to be accepted
at any cost. He took to bribing his neighbors: rice
cakes once a week, flowers to plant because he
bought too many, Japanese music records, and
odd lengths of expensive cloth that were left
over.

Edwards said, "I tell you that boy has that
chutzpah that Sol talks about. He sure as hell has
more guts than me."

Over time, the newlyweds were slowly accepted. Even Mr. Ito, a reclusive old man living

in the largest house in the small community, nodded amiably when he met the couple. He didn't pay attention, at least outwardly, to Montez and his friend. All in all, Montez thought Shelby to be as happy as anyone in love could be.

The house became a home away from home for Shelby's three buddies. They could hardly wait to walk into the little house, as they called it, and to sit on "their" tatami-covered back porch, drink Shelby's beer and discuss philosophy, books, and women—not necessarily in that order. Mariko's round face lit up when her husband's friends visited, no matter what time it was. Her gold tooth, which she was proud of, sparkled as she beamed, "Ohayo gozaimasu, Montez-san, Edwards-san, Sol-san." She always added with an impish look, "Skoshi biru-ne?" as we took off our shoes and donned kimonos.

Montez pretended to be insulted. "Never hoppen, Mariko-san, tokusan biru. You number one girl, biru for Montez-san, no biru for Edwards-san. He no good boy. Wakarimasu ka?"

"Mariko-san" Edwards replied, "Edwards-san have two beers. Wetback friend who swam big river to find many girls, have no biru." Mariko would cover her face with her hands and run giggling to "our" refrigerator.

"We shore got it made, son. Living in tall cotton." Edwards, looking up at the clear blue sky, sighed as he took his first swallow of cold beer. "Ah told you that if you listen to yore pappy, you would be living like a white man."

Montez prepared to eat a feast of soba and beer. "You dumb ridge runner; what would your Blackfoot grand mammy, or whatever Injun you said she was, say if she knew you were living like a white man? You ran around half naked in those hills and didn't own a pair of shoes until Uncle Sammy gave you some."

Sol covered his ears, "Can't you guys keep it down. I'm trying to communicate with my creator and also relax."

Edwards leaned over to Montez and whispered, "Sol is writing stuff about us in that notebook he takes everywhere. I think he's going to include us in his book,

"How in the hell do you know?" Montez asked. "You been sneaking around his stuff?"

"I just picked up the book. He leaves it out in the open, like he doesn't care who sees it."

"Well, we'll see." Montez turned to Sol and loudly asked, "Sol, are you including us in that book you said you are going to write someday?"

"Yep. I figured one of you would read my notes, so I waited until you got curious." Sol added, "I knew you guys wouldn't care, especially if they make a movie and you're in it."

"Do we get any royalties or whatever you call them," Edwards added. "I want to be the handsome hero. Montez will be my faithful servant and companion."

"Don't even try to answer that Sol. Maybe you can have a large dumb dog in the book and name him Ed."

Mariko listened to the three airmen from a safe distance. She couldn't understand why these best of friends talked to each other like that. Strange Americans, but she loved them anyway.

The airmen sat on the porch drinking beer, watching the softly swaying trees and the newly planted chrysanthemums and marigolds.

Shelby stretched contentedly and pointed to his garden, "I don't know why I planted those kind of flowers...they grow in Boston and don't belong here. But, I do."

Montez knew that Shelby had no love for Boston or anyplace else but this cottage. His friends didn't feel sorry for him anymore because of his "physical" problems. In fact, they envied his happy home and having all the money he would ever need.

They constantly reminded him that he had some wonderful friends. Edwards liked to pat him on the back and say, "Boy, you are one fortunate young'un with good buddies to keep that nasty ol' beer from going bad."

One day, sitting on their porch, Edwards, after a long silence said, "You know, I've been hearing some scuttlebutt about Shelby and Mariko. Some of my buddies said Easley and those ol' boys he hangs with are seriously bad-mouthing them."

"What do you mean badmouthing them?" Montez asked. He forced his gaze from the dark green trees and the neat wooden houses nestled among them.

"That fat pig has been going on about how ugly Shelby is and his gook wife. How he gives her money and lives better than white people."

Montez replied, "Hell Ed, all that redneck is…is jealous because Shelby is filthy rich."

Edwards turned to Montez. "I'm not kidding; there may be some trouble."

Edwards' voice sounded serious, and Montez noted he was not using his "down-home" accent. He started to listen and after a while got a bad feeling in his stomach. He knew that Easley could rile up his buddies in no time. Easley would rant and rave about Shelby's marriage to anyone who would listen, especially when Edwards and Montez were within hearing distance. Easley harangued his ground crew about that "rich, ugly Yankee and that gook whore he married." His snide remarks about Mexicans and other ethnics were muted because Montez was part of his ground crew, but he would go on about foreigners and how the purity of the white race was being sullied. The ground crew members made coarse remarks about his views and moved away from him.

"Jesus Christ, Easley's on his rampage again." Lindstrom added. I'm going to the Operations shack to get some Cokes."

"That son of a bitch sure doesn't like anybody," Minnetti replied. "I guess my old man is one of those foreigners he talks about." To them,

Easley was a fool and harmless. But many believed as Easley did and not all were Southerners.

Easley's hatred of Negroes and Jews was extreme, but Montez didn't know how deep it was toward Orientals. Sol recognized Easley's anti-Semitic feelings the first time he met him in the Operations shack.

After Montez told Sol of their conversation about Easley's feelings and their concern regarding Shelby and Mariko, he replied, "I'm surprised that you think I didn't know of his hatred and paranoia." He added with a hint of a smile, "A Jew always knows; they've had hundreds of years of practice."

Later, the three airmen decided to talk about it only in the barracks. "I have a feeling that Shelby may know more about Easley than he lets on," Sol said, "but he hasn't said a word about it." Nevertheless, Shelby and Mariko were not to know until they decided what to do.

There was an understanding that at least one of them was to be at the house. Even at night, if possible. Montez found that he enjoyed visiting alone. After Mariko ensured that he had everything he needed, she would leave him with his book. When he tired of reading, he'd help Mariko in the garden or in the kitchen. There were flowers everywhere, even between the neat rows of cabbages and tomatoes. Montez hadn't paid attention to flowers before, but after Mariko told quaint stories about how they came to have their colors and petals, he saw beauty in every one of them — especially the native brilliant red hibiscus that was used in soothing teas and spells.

He finally met the reticent Mr. Ito, one of the more affluent neighbors, and found him to have a wealth of information about the local plants and wildlife.

In time, to everyone's amazement, Montez became friends with Mr. Ito; and every day, after checking in with Mariko, Montez would stay a few hours at his house. Montez knew he had an affinity with language and easily increased his knowledge of the Japanese/Okinawan language with Mr. Ito's help. Mr. Ito, a martial arts instructor, found Montez to be interested in Okinawan history and culture.

"Ah, Monty-san like Okinawa people? We no same Japanese."

"Mr. Ito, I like Okinawa people and their history." Montez pointed to some herbs and plants Mr. Ito cultivated, "I'd like to know which plants you use for medicine. I saw you use some with Mrs. Katsuno, the sick lady next door. My father's people in Mexico also use medicine like that."

Every foreigner Mr. Ito met, including the Japanese, looked down on the Okinawans. Finding him interested in the martial arts, Mr. Ito took Montez under his wing, teaching him their history with an emphasis on Okinawan Karate-do or Kempo, a synthesis of Chinese Kung-Fu,

Aikijujitsu and secret Okinawan fighting techniques. Montez had studied martial arts for over two years, but found he knew next to nothing. He practiced Kempo every moment he could, but he knew he would never be an expert. He was very interested in their history, especially why their rulers prohibited weapons. He read that Napoleon, in 1816, upon learning of a nation with no weapons, remarked, "I cannot understand a people not interested in war." What Napoleon didn't know was that the martial art of the trained human body became the entire weapon a man needs for self-defense, and offense, if required.

When Montez started to tire, Mr. Ito with his customary stern look, repeatedly reminded him that he would have to study seriously for years to become proficient and an entire lifetime to become a master.

"You work harder. Too tired, no good. Pay attention."

The two Okinawan students never seemed to tire, and Montez felt ashamed. "I'm not tired, Mr. Ito. Please continue."

Sometimes Edwards and Sol visited. "Ah tell you, son, you have gone completely Asiatic. Hell, you bow better than they do."

"I've learned a lot, Ed. It's more than physical effort. I'm learning about our culture, although I live in two cultures, from studying his. I'm learning to focus on the present moment, not live in the past or future."

Edwards turned to Sol. "Can you believe that fool! He's a glutton for punishment. That old man is beating the piss out of him; and he's talking about past and future — I tell you, he's gone Asiatic."

Sol just sucked on his pipe and looked bemused. "Well, he has gotten more muscle on that skinny frame. And it looks like he has gotten that inch he wanted so much, to be over six feet tall... and he seems to be enjoying the battering to some extent."

"And another thing," Edwards said. "What do you mean you live in two cultures?"

Montez felt like wet rag after the session but managed to respond. "Look you dumb hillbilly, at least I'm learning something; however, I'll try to teach you something. I live in our American culture, but I'm influenced immensely by the Mexican culture I learned from my family. I guess you could also say I lived in a third — a 'culture of poverty.' You should know about it, Ed, that's your culture too." Montez added, "I'm just trying to take the best of all of them and come up with something new for me."

"I told you, Sol, that boy is going off his rocker. I'm sorry I asked."

"Try it Ed. I think you'll like it. You should at least try some of the 'Kata.' It's just a sequence of moves... some blocks, stances and strikes."

"You all doing jus' that? Boy, I could of graduated from college with all that time you been doing that there Kata."

Edwards enjoyed making sarcastic comments. "Hot damn, the old man just kicked your ass. Boy, you're twice his size and he throws you around like a baby!"

"Come on, Ed. You can do it. He'll just twist your pencil neck like a pretzel."

Edwards felt it wasn't too smart to be beaten up by a man barely five feet tall. He thought it wouldn't look proper for someone six-feet six-inches tall, to be beaten to a pulp by a midget. However, he got interested in "the art of the empty hand," particularly when he learned that Mr. Ito was trained by a famous karate master in Shuri-te and had continued his studies, even during the big war.

"Monty, you know, this ol' boy is really an expert. Mariko says he's well known."

Edwards started to pester Mr. Ito for some "little ol' lessons" until he finally accepted Edwards as a semi-student, just to quiet him during the sessions with Montez. Also, he could use the money the young men paid and the extra money Shelby donated for needed equipment and special clothing.

As time went by, Mr. Ito's house became as familiar as Shelby's. Montez received most of his training in the Dojo, a martial arts training hall, about fourteen by twenty feet, which took up half the house. The nearly bare room contained reed floor mats, a large, worn, leather punching/kicking bag and a movable closet full of free weights, equipment, thick kimonos and a locked door in a corner. The kitchen, living room, and small bedroom were also bare except for the essential low table and cushions. The house fit Mr. Ito's life style.

The three airmen became permanent fixtures in the small village and were accepted by the neighbors with bows and large smiles in the morning, "Ohayo gozaimasu, Monty-san, Edwards-san." They had more time on their hands as the air war seemed to be slowing down. Sol and Shelby had more of eight-to-five jobs and were stuck at their workplace during the day.

They couldn't tell if Mr. Ito was annoyed or happy to see them. However, during their training sessions, Mr. Ito kept close control of them, particularly Edwards. Montez knew that he would not allow his Okinawan students to behave like them or rest as often. Mr. Ito addressed every situation with a stern, if fragmented, lecture on responsibility, honor and respect. He lectured Edwards like a child due to his cheerful demeanor and constant horseplay when he should have been looking stern, respectful and obedient. Mr. Ito also believed, or at least proclaimed, that Edwards' poor coordination and long legs precluded him from being anything but a buffoon. Edwards tried all the harder to be graceful with his long frame and did noticeably improve his movements and gangly gallop when walking.

During one particularly exhausting morning of relearning how to twist and fall, newly promoted airman 1st Class Shelby burst into the room, "I'm going to be a father! I can't believe it; I'm going to have a baby!" He was exuberant, rushing from one end of the large room to the other. Finally, Mr. Ito sternly instructed him to sit and drink some tea.

Shelby finally calmed down enough to sit on the tatami mat. The group then celebrated the event with a solemn tea ceremony that Mr. Ito had taught them. He felt that his barbarian students would become a little more civilized if they learned to drink tea properly. During the celebration, the young men suddenly remembered that they should congratulate the mother-to-be.

Mariko met them with a huge smile. After being manhandled with their congratulations, she left, flustered and happy, to get her guests some biru for a long celebration. When everyone had a beer, Shelby raised his hand for silence. "I want to thank you guys for your friendship and everything you have done for us...."

"Shell, you got it backwards," Montez interjected. "You're the one we should...."

"Please. Please, let me continue. Because you are my friends, I'm going to ask even more of you. I need all of you to promise to take care of Mariko and my child if anything should happen to me. By the way, she is over three months pregnant. I have talked to my lawyer in Boston, and he is preparing papers to transfer a trust fund in my name to Mariko and my child. Monty, you have been named executor. I know what you're going to say, but I know you have always wanted to be an attorney and you will be. The trust is rather large so you are going to have to be on the ball."

"Shell, you're crazy as hell. Nothing's going to happen to you, and besides I don't even like lawyers."

Edwards tried to lighten up the now somber gathering by putting his arms around Shelby and Montez. "Monty will make a good shyster lawyer and take care of everything. And don't worry; I'm going to watch him all the time with all that money."

Sol asked, "Why are you bringing this up at this particular time, Shelby? I recognize you have new responsibilities, but why are you so specific about something happening to you?"

Shelby stood up and walked to the end of the room, looked at them for a long minute and returned. You fellows think I don't know why one of you is always here or at Mr. Ito's house? I know you'd rather be drinking beer and having fun at the New Ginza. I've heard the rumors. In fact, I've been called names and accosted by some people. I don't want to go into details. I can handle that."

"Do you mean physically accosted?" Sol asked.

Shelby started for the door and turned. "Look, I don't want to discuss it. You can't do anything about it. You're doing everything you can do...no, much more than anyone could expect. I thank you again for everything and...I'm going to see Mariko."

Mr. Ito couldn't follow the conversation, but knew there was a change in the young men.

"What hoppen? Mariko dai jobu desu ka...is she okay?"

"She's fine, Mr. Ito," replied Montez, "You should know some bad soldiers don't want Shelby-san married to Mariko. They might hurt Shelby-san."

Mr. Ito's concerned face turned stern, "They don't like him marry Okinawa girl? You want I watch her?"

"Yes, please watch both of them," said a concerned Sol. "But don't let Shelby-san know we asked you to."

Montez added, "Also, don't let Mariko know anything is wrong. She has enough to do with having a baby."

Edwards stopped his pacing. "If any of those peckerheads hurt these two, I'll kill them."

Chapter 10

Changes

Mariko was beginning to really show. She made sure Montez noticed her stomach bulge and waited for his comment.

"Baby show tokusan, ne?

"The baby is very big Mariko. Pretty soon come out to see uncle Montez-san. You look very pretty with your nice yellow dress."

Mariko smiled, satisfied, and walked Montez to his favorite spot on the porch. She had a different color western-style maternity dress for each day of the week and paraded for her neighbors every morning under the guise of working the garden. The older women were still a little standoffish, but the young ones commented on her pretty dresses and her good fortune.

The visits were still relaxing for Montez; however, a new element was present. He was worried for her and Shelby. He absently walked to the window every few minutes to check on Mariko instead of listening to Mr. Ito's instructions.

"You no pay attention. You think too much about Mariko. No worry, neighbors watch Mariko too. Kanji and Kichiro also watch. None hurt her."

Somewhat mollified, Montez paid attention to Mr. Ito. The days passed with no incidents, but his demeanor communicated his feeling to Mariko.

"Montez-san, why you not happy? You have long face and not smile all time like before. Edwards-san and Sol-san not happy long time too. Edwards-san follow me all time. I pushed him outside house. Told him go play with Mr. Ito."

Montez smiled picturing Edwards and Mr. Ito playing ball. "I'm happy, Mariko. I just have work on my mind."

Mariko was more assertive with Montez and his friends. She would insist her way was the proper way in doing things. He teased her by insisting she couldn't tell right from wrong. She knew that he teased her but couldn't help but respond. Her old friends didn't visit her. Montez figured they wouldn't feel comfortable in this neighborhood, and besides, she now lived a different life and was a different person. Some local young women did visit her, if only out of curiosity. Mariko was happy with her new friends. She was also coming into her own in the neighborhood. Happiness radiated throughout her body: shining, eager eyes, red cheeks and a bounce to her movements despite the heaviness in her stomach — pregnancy became her. Shelby, in his own heaven, watched her with a smile on his gaunt face as if he couldn't believe his good luck.

Montez and his friends fretted even more now that Mariko's stomach was large with child. They were in a different world with her — flowers and peace — an island of serenity. At the base, they had the uncertainty of the aircrew's safety, constant work on their aircraft and Easley's railing against anyone different from him. Montez no longer went off base to relax. The village was no longer a playground to drink and find girls. He saw a different picture when he and Edwards sporadically visited the village: garish signs on dilapidated shacks, loud soldiers, sad dehumanized women making merry to satisfy their customers and owners. He wanted to feel like he did when he saw his first village full of girls — a See's Candy boy.

"I think we've been here too long," Montez said morosely. "I can't have fun anymore until we get away from the village and out to the bush. Do you think we're getting too old?"

Work and visiting Shelby and Mariko's house passed pleasantly for a couple of month. Montez' hours at the base were constant, almost like peacetime.

The winding down air war suddenly came to life. The Chinese communists were playing politics with peace. Many of the dormant bombers were soon flying missions again. American leaders thought this would force the Chinese to the bargaining table at Panmunjom. The bombers were once again flying into MiG alley but not suffering with the previous heavy loses. The Air Force F-86 Saber jet fighters with superior pilots had cleared out the Chinese MiGs for all practical purposes, and the B-29s could again fly with acceptable losses. The war continued and Montez lost all expectations of going home early.

"Goddamned Air Force should have let them Saber jets fight here months ago. Look how many '29s they shot down. Those old Air Force and Navy jets couldn't do anything against them MiG-15 and Roosian pilots."

"If you air war experts are finished," said Sol, "perhaps you can let me know when you're getting off base. I haven't been off for a week."

"Hell if I know when we get off," answered Montez. "This can go on for a long time or something can happen at the talks, or to the plane, and we could be off tomorrow."

Sol was the only one who could leave the base fairly regularly to see Mariko and then for only a few hours. The Operations room was busy with an influx of visitors and aircraft. Montez and Edwards saw Shelby at the supply shack whenever they could.

They met in Sol's spartan room to discuss Mariko and Shelby. Sol's three roommates were out.

"For Christ's sake, Sol, " said Montez, relishing the Christian remark, as he looked around a room where shoes and uniforms were neatly placed and beds tightly made. "This place looks like no one lives here."

"Just because it's not a pig pen like you grease monkeys live in doesn't mean it's not comfortable," replied Sol, getting an ashtray for Edwards' cigarette, but making sure it was also next to Montez who was learning to smoke. "But let's get down to business."

"I'm worried about Shelby," said Montez. "He doesn't seem at all his old self. Does anyone know if he's been pushed around or threatened?"

"I haven't heard anything," replied Sol, knocking Edwards long legs and dirty brogans off the neat bunk.

"Me neither," said Montez. "But something is wrong, although I see no change in Mariko. She's beginning to look like she swallowed a basketball."

Montez was surprised that Edwards didn't spout some corny remark, but he hadn't been himself for over a month. Who would have believed that Edwards was the sparkplug of the group. You expected his county sayings and quipping. Montez didn't like the changes in them—in all of them.

"All I know," said Edwards as he paced the little room, "is that ol' Easley is full of himself and joking with his friends in a way I don't like."

"What do you mean?"

"Well, he says things like they're going to kick his ass, and I know they mean Shelby. But what really bothers me is his snide comments about Mariko. I'm sure they're talking about her. He's saying they're going to run that whore out of town and back where she belongs. Who else could they possibly mean?"

"The worst of it all," said Montez angrily, "while Ed and I are working, Easley sometimes changes shifts with Sergeant Pappas. Who knows what he does during that time."

"Let's try to not worry too much." Sol cut in. "Mariko's neighbors and Mr. Ito watch over her. And those two Okinawan lads training with Mr. Ito could take on twice their number if it came to that."

"I'm not too tense," answered Montez with a grin. "I'm just alert. Anyway, I'm not worried about daytime. What about at night?" Montez fidgeted with a well-worn cap. "Someone could break in, tear up the place and no one would know."

"I think we are making up ghosts," said Sol, trying to calm them down. "Shelby can take care of himself and if anything happened, they'd scream to high heaven."

"You're right," sighed Montez. "Maybe we're getting paranoid and seeing ghosts, as you say. We'll be getting off base soon. This push will slow down as soon as the North Koreans see it's no use arguing over nothing and getting bombed."

"I hope you guys are right," Edwards finally said. "Y'all know a little paranoia is good. Someone's always after you one way or another."

A few days after their meeting, the bombing of North Korea slowed down with new negotiations at Panmunjom. The "Pesky Fly" was finally getting a well-deserved rest and a looking over. The ground crew discussed where and how they were going to spend their time. Montez, Edwards and Sol decided that the first one off duty would immediately go to see Mariko. Continued aircraft maintenance kept them on base for several more days; however, Sol would see Mariko in the evenings every two or three days.

"She's fine, you guys," said Sol after one of his trips. "Shelby seems much more relaxed now so I think you fellows ought to lighten up."

"Great, "Montez replied, "Now I have some news. I overheard Sergeant Pappas tell Major Cunningham that the 'Pesky Fly' is about as ready as she'll ever be. So I believe we're going to get off in a couple days."

"From your lips to the ears of God," replied Sol, tapping his cruddy pipe on a very clean ashtray."

The duty schedule was posted on the tattered bulletin board assigning Edwards first round of aircraft guard duty. The rest of the ground crew was free until time for guard duty. Edwards didn't mind night guard duty except when he went through the aircraft—he was too tall to walk through the compartments, so he crouched, sometimes on his knees, on his way through the plane.

"I'm off for at least two days starting tomorrow, according to the schedule," announced a jubilant Montez. "I'm heading out to see Mariko early."

Montez enjoyed the sunny, cloudless Saturday morning, relishing the feeling of freedom while bouncing his way in a pedicab to Mariko's little house. Strange that we never thought of it as Shelby's house, he thought. He deeply breathed the peculiar but not unpleasant smell that was Okinawa: generous layers of manure; food, especially fried tofu and fish; the ubiquitous outhouses; rotting vegetation; all mixed well by the gentle sea breeze. The day was young and crisp, and he let the sun bathe his face. Coming up to the village, a jeep and the back end of a car, partially hidden by a house, jutted out. Then he saw several more official-looking cars, and finally, APs and Okinawan policemen swarming over the normally quiet village. Montez felt a sinking feeling in his stomach and then panic. He ran to Mariko's house and collided with a large Okinawan policeman who held him while summoning an AP.

"My friend lives in that house!" Montez yelled to an AP sergeant. "What happened?"

"Take it easy, sergeant. What's your friend's name?"

After a long explanation, they finally allowed him access. "You can go in the house when they're finished," the Lieutenant said. "Let us know if you see anything stolen or unusual but don't touch anything."

Mr. Ito stood in front of Mariko's house. Montez didn't see any of the other neighbors and hurried to Mr. Ito's side.

"I heard loud noise of crashing, wake up, and went to see!" said a shaken Mr. Ito. "Too late, bad GIs gone. Shelby-san on ground out-side door. He bent over. I turn over and he no have face left. Can't see for blood. Eye pop out of face a little. Blood on wall, on ground. Every-where in room."

Montez squatted Okinawan-style near the front door listening to Mr. Ito's story, his head in his hands. He absently noted small pools of blood drying, feeding the flowers planted by Mariko not more than two months ago. Three black ants scurried about looking for food, care-fully skirting the blood.

Mr. Ito added hopefully, "Shelby-san alive. I felt and he breathes."

"Where is Mariko?" Montez asked for the third time as he heavily got to his feet and started to pace. "Someone must have seen her."

"Mariko gone. Back door open, nobody in house. I don't know, Montez-san. I find, later."

Montez felt something missing from Mr. Ito's voice. He didn't seem too concerned over Mariko. Normally, Mr. Ito watched over Mariko like she was his daughter. He put it out of his mind and went to talk to the investigating lieu-tenant where he heard a similar report.

"I haven't seen anyone beat up this bad.

Now, do you know who would do this? Nothing was taken according to his neighbor, Mr. Ito."

"Yeah, I know someone who might do this. I don't know how it can be proved, but I know of at least one guy."

"OK, I want to talk to you at length. I'm Lieutenant Connors and we'll need a complete statement."

The lieutenant watched Montez's dejected face. "I'm sorry. I hope he makes it. Get more info on your friend at the base hospital. You can go inside the house now but don't move anything. We may need to take more pictures. Don't forget; if anything's missing let me know."

The lieutenant led Montez into the porch area and stood patiently by the door watching him walk through the house. Montez found the normally immaculate room leading to the front door in shambles. The flimsy wood and paper walls were splintered and torn. Blood was spattered on the entrance area and on some of the scattered shoes that were once neatly lined up outside the sliding door. He carefully searched the front room for anything that could help him tie in Sergeant Easley or his buddies. Nothing. The rest of the house he knew so well appeared as if Mariko just cleaned it. Montez searched the closet and found all of Mariko's clothing there; she apparently left in a hurry not taking anything with her. There was a large amount of script, eighty-seven dollars, on a small table. This was obviously not about money or material gain. It was also obvious that the encounter was only in the entryway to the house.

Montez walked out of the house and saw the APs and Okinawan police trampling Mariko's flowers and shrubs.

"Hey! You guys!" Montez yelled. "Can you destroy any more evidence with your big feet? Do you have to stomp all over the garden before you're finished?"

He stalked off before anyone replied, surprised that he chewed out some officers and the police. Montez stopped at Mr. Ito's house, quickly glanced back and saw the lieutenant looking at him. Hell with them.

"Mr. Ito, I'm leaving now, but will be back tonight after I see Shelby-san at the hospital. Please look for Mariko. She has to be nearby with friends or maybe with family. I know she said she didn't have any, but I know she must."

"I find Mariko. Don't you worry, Montez-san; no one hurt her."

Montez studied Mr. Ito's face and his tone of voice…the old fox obviously had her hidden away.

Returning to the base, the sky was neither as blue nor the weather as invigorating as before. Montez was afraid of what he would find at the hospital and dreaded telling Edwards and Sol about Shelby and Mariko. Everything they feared, but didn't believe would happen, happened.

Chapter 11

Waiting

The base hospital was housed in a modern building, which gave Montez hope for Shelby's medical care. He quickly walked into the somber, cool corridor and couldn't see for a moment, then found the nurse receptionist and asked for Shelby. She requested the patients last name; Montez couldn't remember — he had always called him by his first name. "I believe his last name is Stone, no Wellstone, Sergeant Shelby Wellstone. He was brought in four or five hours ago."

"I'm sorry, Sergeant, you can't see him now. No visitors according to his chart. He just came out of surgery two hours ago." The nurse pointed to an officer coming out of a door. "There's his doctor now. You can ask him about your friend."

Montez hurried to the officer, all the while trying to decide whether to call him doctor or major. "I'm Sergeant Montez, Doctor. I'm here to inquire about Sergeant Shelby Wellstone. I've been delegated by his friends to find out his condition."

After seeing the doctor's reluctance to give out information, Montez added, with a stretch, "I was told by Lieutenant Connors, the military police investigator in charge of this case, to secure as much information on Sergeant Wellstone as I can. I'm to give a report as soon as possible."

Upon hearing that the police directed him to the hospital for information, the doctor took Montez to his spartan office; a yellow writing pad and sharp orange pencil sat atop a barewood desktop. "Your friend is in a coma. He has taken a severe beating. We performed surgery on his left eye and had to suture the deep lacerations on his face, head and on a torn ear. In addition, there are broken ribs and sundry cuts and bruises on his shoulders, arms and legs. However, those are not critical. I'm worried about the coma he is in. He must have put up some fight."

"Is he going to be all right? I mean when will he come out of the coma?"

"Look, Sergeant, let me give it to you straight. We don't know when, or if, he's going to make it. His vital signs are stable, but he is in serious condition. "The blows to his head caused his brain to swell due to leakage from blood vessels. When the brain swells, it has no room to expand in the skull, which leads to a rise in pressure within the brain. In some cases, removal of small amounts of fluid from the brain may be beneficial … I can go on, but let it suffice that a person in a coma doesn't react to reflexive or conscious movement. When a person begins to emerge from the coma, he reacts to certain stimuli. Let's hope that happens; we'll be watching for it. If he comes out of the coma, he may have retrograde amnesia. He probably won't know who did this to him for a while. We have called in a specialist from Japan, and perhaps we'll know more in a couple days."

Montez had a hundred questions to ask, but before he could start, the doctor asked him. "Do you know whom we can contact? We haven't received his 201 file."

"Yes sir. He's from Boston and his parents are there. He also has a wife in the village not far from the base."

"A wife … in the village? How can he have a wife? Do you mean a girlfriend?"

"No sir. A wife. They were married about eight months ago by an Okinawan priest. Sergeant Wellstone sent the paperwork to his CO and his attorney in Boston to make it legal, and I was named executor. And she is going to have a baby soon."

"Well, I've never heard of such a thing. An attorney, you say?"

"Shelby is not an ordinary airman, sir. He's a millionaire and has friends in high places." Montez thought he might as well go all the way, "He and his family are well known in the social and political circles in Massachusetts."

"The doctor shook his head and muttered. "A pregnant wife — in the village."

"Can I see him, doctor?"

"Not now. Come back tomorrow and maybe you can see him for a minute; however, he won't know you're there."

Montez left the hospital in a daze. The bright sun blinded him when he stepped out of the dark hospital entrance. Sitting on a bench under a tree, his mind felt dull and his head ached. A coma...Shelby might not come out of it. After a while, he got up, slowly walked to his barracks and stopped at the PX to get some food. He hadn't eaten since yesterday and figured he needed his strength for what he had to do. Edwards should be awake by now after guard duty, he thought. Sol should be on duty at Operations for another two hours.

After he finished an unsavory ham and cheese sandwich soaked in mayonnaise, his pace picked up and he began to get angry. Wild thoughts flashed through his mind. Montez abruptly stopped. Easley must have some cuts and bruises. The lieutenant and doctor said there must have been a hard fight. He had to see Easley now, and he needed a camera.

He ran most of the way to the barrack and found Edwards toweling himself after a shower. He looked like a giant preying mantis — long tentacle-like arms and legs rubbing its body.

"What the hell you doing here?" asked a surprised Edwards. "You're supposed...."

"Ed, shut up and listen." Montez waited for Edwards to stop sputtering.

"Shelby was beat up last night and is in the base hospital. I just returned from there, and he's in a coma. Mariko is missing."

Montez then waited for the inevitable questions he couldn't answer.

"What do you mean, beat up? Is he going to be all right? Where's Mariko?" Edwards spouted. "What the hell is being done?"

Montez put his hands up to stop his questions and related what he knew of the attack. "Mr. Ito, and I'm sure the rest of the village, will be looking for Mariko. I feel that Mr. Ito knows more than he's letting on. Hell, if I were him, I'd keep her away from the police and the military. That way she'd be safe from whomever did this."

Edwards tripped over his khaki trousers in his haste, unable to put his long legs into the pant legs. "We got to find out who did this and also find Mariko. Shit, we know who did this, and I'm going to put him in a coma!"

"Take it easy, Ed. I felt the same way walking over from the hospital, but we have to think about it first. Let's talk to Sol, but first let me tell you my plan. We find that bastard and any of his friends who might be in on it. You know who they may be more than Sol or I do. Then check them out for bruises and cuts. Hell, Shelby put up a good fight, and they're probably banged up some. We'll take pictures of them if they're cut up."

"Let's do it now before they can take care of any bruises," said Edwards as he hurriedly tucked the blouse into his pants. "I want to give them more than little bumps. I wish I had brass knuckles or something 'cause if we try to take pictures of them, we're in for a fight."

"Ed, you wouldn't know what to do with brass knuckles. You gotta promise me something. I get Easley. You can have anyone else. OK?"

"Okay. Just don't forget he outweighs you by fifty pounds. Just because he's a fat ass doesn't mean he's not strong as an ox."

They took the first 6x6 truck available to the flight line but couldn't find Easley. Sergeant Pappas was, as always, with his plane.

"He left yesterday and I don't expect him for at least three days." The sergeant looked quizzically at them. "Anything I can do?"

"No thanks, Sarge," said Edwards. "Just needed something I lent him. See you."

They left Sergeant Pappas with a quizzical look on his face. The sergeant knew they would never look for Easley unless something extraordinary had happened. They stopped to see Sol. He was shocked speechless when told what happened to Shelby and Mariko. They agreed to meet in his room in an hour. Before Sol could ask any questions, they dashed out of the Operations shack.

"Let's start at Easley's place first," said Montez. "We may luck out and find the son-of-a-bitch and his stupid buddies."

They separated and went into the barracks from both entrances hoping to catch Easley. The storm shutters were closed in each large room, dimming the area where tired airmen were getting as much sleep as possible. They found Easley's room vacant except for an old snoring sergeant in his bunk.

"Christ's sake, that guy sounds like a '29 engine. Come on," said Edwards, pulling on his friend's arm. "I know where his buddies are."

They quickly went to the enlisted men's barracks and entered, careful to cover both exits of the barracks. Their bunks were empty.

Edwards scanned the rooms. "Those rednecks wouldn't have left such neat rooms unless they planned to be away for awhile. Where in the hell can they be?"

They searched the room for any indication of their whereabouts to no avail. They walked out disappointed, not being too careful how they left the area.

"Hell with it," said Montez. "Let's go see Sol."

They found Sol nervously pacing his room. "Where in the hell have you been? I thought you left to look for Mariko without me."

"Easy Sol," said Montez. "Let's go to the hospital to see how Shelby is. Maybe they will let us see him. I doubt it, but we can try."

The three airmen walked rapidly to the hospital discussing Easley and his cronies, oblivious to the scorching sun and the distance to their destination, their uniforms wet with sweat. Ideas as to Easley and company's whereabouts came furiously and were as quickly discarded. They finally admitted that they had no idea where Easley or his cohorts could be hiding, much less who they were. They knew, however, that Easley would not be with his friends — it would be too stupid to be found together; and Easley, while not intelligent, was a wily man.

The hospital nurse updated Shelby's condition — no change.

"I'm sorry, but you can't see him now. Maybe tomorrow, but you have to talk to the doctor first."

Dejected, they walked out of the hospital. Montez suggested, "Let's go to the Air Police headquarters; maybe we can get a report on what they've found so far."

"Do you believe they will tell us anything regarding their investigation?" asked Sol, his skeptical voice answering his question. "Who knows, they may even suspect us. We were at his house constantly which may give them cause to question our motives."

"I don't know," said Montez, rubbing his chin reflectively. "Anyway I have to give them a statement, and I suspect they will want one from you guys."

They walked into police headquarters with trepidation. It was a modified Quonset hut with three rooms separated by eight-foot partitions, a raised desk near the entrance and two wooden benches. They had nothing to hide but still didn't quite trust the police — even if they wore khaki like themselves.

"I'm Sergeant Montez. I'm here to see Lieutenant Connors about a beating incident in the village last night. He wants me to give a statement."

The air policeman, a tall extremely thin corporal, escorted Montez to the lieutenant's door. He walked back to the front desk and gave Sol and Edwards a long, accusatory look. Edwards and Sol sitting on a bench, shifted uncomfortably.

Finally, Sol got up and told the morose AP, who listened with his thin neck craned forward, "I believe that the lieutenant will also want a statement from us."

The Skull, as he was instantly named by Edwards, seemed to be satisfied with that explanation and returned to his paperwork. Every few minutes he would look up, glare at them in a birdlike manner, then return to his work.

"The Skull reminds me of a vulture waiting to feed at the first sign of weakness," whispered Edwards. "Christ, what is Montez doing in there — writing a dang book?"

"Quiet! He can hear us and we don't want any trouble from him now. John ought to be out pretty soon."

Montez was anxious to leave, but Lieutenant Connors kept repeating some of the questions in different ways. Guess he's trying to trip me up, thought Montez, but he really is too obvious. The lieutenant was friendly enough, although he wouldn't reveal any information regarding his investigation other than the obvious. Perhaps the lieutenant didn't know anymore than he did — probably less because the neighbors wouldn't talk to him. Montez described Easley, his friends and what he thought might have happened, then surreptitiously asked some questions of his own.

"Well, I told Shelby he was buying into trouble when he married an Okinawan girl. You know some people don't like that."

"This isn't the first time this kind of thing has happened." The Lieutenant stretched, lit a cigarette, and relaxed after completing the interview. "I've had cases where people have sliced each other up — of course, these were between colored folk and white soldiers. Not much you can do about it. Just soldiers fighting among themselves like they always do. Not too much different than this, except your friend married one of them. Just looking for trouble."

"Well, you're right there, sir. I told him what could happen. But now that this happened, what would the Air Force do to the men who did it?"

"Probably not much, Sergeant. Maybe Sergeant Easley would loose a stripe, at the most. That is, of course, if his court martial finds him guilty... if there is a court martial. There's a war on you know, and he's needed on his aircraft."

"But what if something really bad happens to Sergeant Wellstone?" Montez couldn't say "dead."

"We'll do everything possible to find the men who did this. Have you even considered that he may have been attacked by Okinawans?"

"Yes sir. I've considered it, and I know it wasn't them."

"All right. I may want to talk to you later. Please send in Sergeant Edwards."

Edwards, hearing the request relayed to the corporal by Montez, popped off the bench like a jack-in-the-box relieved to be doing something and getting away from the Skull.

Walking to the bench, Montez looked at his watch and found he had been with the lieutenant for over an hour and a half. His wait in front of the Skull was not long. Edwards was out in fifteen minutes and Sol in even less time.

Montez told his friends what he told the lieutenant and the replies from the questions he asked. Sol had very little to report to the lieutenant except to ask how the investigation was progressing.

"All that boy wanted to know is why I was Shelby's friend" muttered Edwards angrily as they walked to the main gate of the base. "And if I really thought Shelby was beat up by my friends. I told that god-damned cop that those peckerheads weren't my friends. I tell you boys those APs aren't going to do a damn thing to find anything."

"For once you're right Ed," said Sol while looking for a pedicab. "Let's search Mariko's house and the surrounding area and talk to the...."

"I want to talk to Mr. Ito," interjected Montez. "He knows more than he let on. I don't care if he trusts us or not; we have to find Mariko. She's got the answers to our questions."

They arrived at Mariko's village as the sun's luminosity lost its glare, slowly slipped behind a distant mountain and left a soft afterglow.

"It's really too late to do much good searching the area," said Sol. He started walking on the well-worn path towards Mariko's house. "John, I think you ought to talk to Mr. Ito alone. We don't want him to think we're ganging up on him."

"OK. I'll see you guys at the house." Montez ambled the short distance to Mr. Ito's house. He couldn't help thinking that just a short time ago, he was happily walking over there to learn a new fighting stance. Now, he didn't know if he was considered a friend or foe.

Mr. Ito was waiting for him, and they greeted each other with a formal bow.

Without waiting for further formalities, Montez asked for Mariko.

"Exuberance of youth not excuse for bad manners, Montez-san."

"Please forgive my rudeness sir, but I'm worried about Mariko." He bowed again, and waited. Chastened, Montez thought how many times he stood like this in front of his father. No, it was different—then he had been afraid of a beating.

"Mariko is with friends and in good health. I take you to her. She ask for you, Edwards-san and Sol-san many times. But I also worry about Shelby-san. Mariko make herself sick. Too much worry."

Montez sighed with relief and said, "Shelby's in bad condition. He has a concussion which is very serious and the doctor isn't sure if he will be OK."

"He will be OK. Come, Montez-san; let us talk to others before big bird step on flowers."

He walked off. Montez stared after him. He didn't believe it—Mr. Ito actually cracked a joke about Edwards. It struck him that the old man didn't do or say things without a reason. Mr. Ito was putting him at ease!

Mr. Ito walked slowly while Montez explained Shelby's condition and what occurred at the police station. They reached the once-flowered walkway to Mariko's house. Montez looked away from the bloodstained entrance— Christ, we have to clean that. They found Edwards and Sol grimly going through each room carefully looking for anything that could help them tie in Easley. They bowed to Mr. Ito. Will miracles ever cease, thought Montez.

After allowing a few words of greeting, Montez broke in, to Mr. Ito's obvious displeasure, "Forget it you guys. I looked around and there's nothing inside the house. Good news though...Mariko is OK. Mr. Ito sent her to stay with some friends."

"Well, that's the best news I've heard in a month of Sundays. We got to talk to her about what happened that night," said Edwards.

"I know I'm abrupt and disrespectful, but I think time is of the essence," said Montez, again risking Mr. Ito's displeasure.

"There never no loss by using small time for manners," countered a frowning Mr. Ito.

"I'm sorry sir. We need to know if Mariko will return to her house. Would she want to live there again?"

"I not know." After a long minute Mr. Ito added, "Fix and clean house and everything be as before. Maybe come back...she very afraid."

"We'll fix the house and...."

"Yeah, we'll replant all the flowers," interjected Edwards. "I'll fix that sliding panel that's stuck and lay some bricks along the pathway like she always wanted." He finally contained his excitement and stopped talking. He looked at his staring friends and indignantly grumbled, "Well...I will."

"Tell her that she doesn't need to be afraid." Montez finally said. "Also, that bad GIs only wanted to hurt Shelby-san, not her. I think it's better not to say how serious Shelby is...only that he will be in the hospital for a long time."

"I hope you're right, John. Sometimes it's best to let one know the truth. Also what makes you think that they won't come after her?" asked Sol.

"Well, I know they're bastards," reflected Montez, "but I think they didn't really want her—just wanted to teach Shelby a lesson. The main reason is Mariko's condition. She's due in a month or so. What do you think, Ed? You know those crackers and how they think."

"I think you're right, Monty. Those ol' boys just wanted to kick ass. They're probably scared shitless right now. They'll stay as far away from this place as they can."

"Another reason I felt she should come home is, well…let's face facts; she will only be accepted elsewhere for a short time." Montez hesitated again, then added, "This is her home, at least for now. We can ensure that she has everything she needs in case the worst happens to Shelby. Also, we're not going to be here forever. We have to talk to that Boston lawyer and the Okinawan lawyer in Naha. We need their help. I'm calling both lawyers tomorrow to get the ball rolling.

"Damn, if that ol' boy doesn't come up with good ideas. I told you that you're wrong, Sol. Monty does have a little brain and it works sometimes."

Sol didn't answer. He shook his head a little, smiling, and pulled out his pipe. Mr. Ito had long ago decided to disregard the tall barbarian.

"I just wonder where those ol' boys went off to." Edwards looked furiously at his audience,

"I bet they know I'm a going to kick their asses when I find them."

Chapter 12

Sergeant Easley

Sergeant Easley slowly shifted his considerable behind on the tatami mat. He needed another beer and looked around the austere well-kept room for his musume. Damn girl is never around when you need her. Maybe I'm paying her too much, and she's getting lazy. The tatami mat was getting hard on him... he better lose some weight, he thought; good living was getting to him.

"Goddemmit, Yoshiko, where the hell are you? Cain't a man git a damned beer when he wants one?"

Then he remembered that he sent her across the village to get him some Camels. Shit, he had already smoked a carton he brought to this godforsaken place. It was a shame that he had to spend his leave in this dump, but he had to get out of circulation for a while.

Easley looked outside at the cloudless sky. It looked like another hot day. He chose this village and house because he could easily see the two roads leading to his house. And the village was as far as he could get from Kadena Air Base. Still, he was bored. His good ol' boys weren't here…at his order, and they weren't told where he holed up. The village was nondescript: dusty brown roads and houses, occasionally festooned with white banners slashed with red Japanese symbols. *At least the other villages have some bars and dances. This place is just a large whorehouse with houses instead of cribs, just like that dump in the Philippines.* Even though it was far from a military or naval base, the place filled up in the evening with soldiers.

Easley stiffened as his gaze dropped to the hard packed road's edge. Two tall GIs, with a third GI hidden behind them, were striding towards the village. He moved quickly for a heavy-set man. *They couldn't have found him way out here,* he thought, but he couldn't take chances. He searched the room for a weapon. Then moved to a window facing the road to get a better look. *Just some soldiers hurrying to get out of the sun, find some beer and a musume.* He sighed with relief.

I got nothing to worry about so why am I watching for those three punks. He sat down on a well-worn wooden chair and found he had been holding his breath. Easley breathed deeply and thought about his predicament.

Don't see why Edwards should care much

for a goddamned Boston Yankee and a gook whore...what's this man's Air Force coming to. The greaser and the Jew boy...well, that's strange too. That wetback better be watched though. He'd probably stick a knife up my ass; that's how they are.

Easley jumped as Yoshiko kicked off her wooden shoes and entered the house. "God-demmit gal, why you'll sneaking up on me like that. I oughtta kick yore skinny ass. Jesus Christ!"

"No have Camels. I find you Lucky Strike cigarette." She looked up at him.

Easley saw she was frightened. He liked her frightened, but not too much. He playfully patted her behind, and she giggled in relief. He thought that's all these musumes need to keep them in line—kick their ass then stroke it a little. He wanted her with him right now and grabbed her.

"Itai! You hurt me, Easy-san."

She tried to pull away rubbing her arm. He pushed her away and paced around the room. He felt cooped up and knew he took it out on her. When he looked out the window again, he saw two girls walking on the path to the house and felt his face turning red with anger.

"Yoshiko, your goddemmed friends are coming over heah again. I don't want those bitches over. An' tell them I'll kick their asses if they show up heah agin. You tell them now."

Easley's angry voice made her cringe. Even to his ears, he sounded strained—high pitched and angry.

"Ojosans only bring sake, Easy-san. You before want sake."

"All right gal," he said remembering. "Tell them to bring me some soba. I'm beginning to git hungry."

He glanced at her. The frightened eyes and quivering lips were still there. He realized that he told her to do things and then yelled at her for doing them. Worrying about that damned Yankee bastard is getting to me, he thought. Screw it, I'm paying her plenty of money, and she's here only for that.

Easley walked again to the window, looked at the hot empty village and felt bile rush to his stomach. I told those ol' boys we only wanted to kick that gook-lover's ass, not kill him. He started to sweat as he remembered that dark night. It was fun and exciting at first sneaking up on the house. Like that time, outside Biloxi, when they stomped that ol' colored man. But this time it was more complicated. Foley was to follow Montez to find Shelby's house, but he should have remembered that ol' Foley was known to spit against the wind and think it's raining. Foley didn't recognize the house in the dark, and they fumbled around until he found it.

Things went wrong immediately. Shelby surprised them sneaking into the house, smashing Whitey's nose as he stepped through the door. Easley remembered that Whitey fell backwards and that stupid Foley walked in and let the god-damn punk hit him in the head. Whitey and Foley acted like some lunatics as they swung wildly at Shelby until he fell. The boys wanted blood, and Easley knew he had to stop them. He remembered their grunts as they repeatedly hit Shelby, and him yelling, "Don't kick him. You'll kill 'im, you stupid assholes!"

Easley finally yanked Foley away; it took both of them to stop Whitey from stomping Shelby's head to a pulp. Whitey's a good ol' boy, but he has a mean temper. Easley then remembered Mariko and ran through the house looking for her. Gone out the back for help, he figured. He rushed out the front door waving at his buddies to follow. They must have run a mile in the dark without stopping. Christ, he couldn't even run a few yards without gasping for breath.

Goddamn it, why did I ever start this in the first place... it just didn't go as planned. The only good thing was that he didn't see me. But what if that whore did? What if that ugly bastard dies? Hell, we only stomped him for a couple minutes. Easley walked away from the window dejectedly shaking his head — things always seem to go wrong for me.

Chapter 13

Legal Action

Mr. Ito accompanied Montez to Naha, Okinawa, to discuss Mariko's situation with Shelby's attorney, Mr. Takahashi.

Montez had not visited Naha for over six months and noted that much of the World War II damage he marveled at earlier was gone. Although the town still had a semi-rural appearance, a modern city's foundation was being laid.

Mr. Takahashi's office was located in a substantial partial-brick building, one of the few left, near the center of town. The large, modern complex teemed with busy people. Mr. Takahashi, a small dapper man with a thin mustache, bowed and showed them into his spacious office, which contained only a large teak desk with a folder on top, a large black sofa and four leather chairs. He ordered tea in perfect English.

"Mr. Takahashi, as you probably know, our primary concern is Mariko's welfare. We would like to know, among other things, if there is enough money for her to live on, and if her house is fully paid?"

"Sergeant Montez, she has more than enough money. The house was bought outright. I also have a personal interest in this case because I like Mariko and Sergeant Wellstone... and this situation intrigues me."

Mr. Takahashi pulled a document from a drawer in his neat desk. "I was instructed by Sergeant Wellstone several months ago to arrange for his attorney in Boston, Mr. Joseph Day, to transfer fifty thousand dollars to his Naha account and give you power of attorney. In addition, Mariko has a large trust fund in the United States under Mr. Day's management. A month ago, Sergeant Wellstone gave me additional instructions regarding Mariko's everyday needs and to insure that she has the best medical care, in case anything happened to him. Sergeant Wellstone was very thorough, and I will give you his instructions, in writing, before you leave."

Mr. Takahashi smiled, "Please don't worry, Sergeant... Mariko is a very rich woman."

Several moments passed until Mr. Ito nudged Montez into a reply. "You mean I take care of Mariko? Does Mariko know this? How do I do this... I mean does she get money from the bank?"

"I know this seems complicated, but basically you have fifty thousand dollars at your immediate disposal, and more if needed. I believe that Sergeant Wellstone told you that you had access to money in case of emergency."

"He told me of some money, but I didn't understand how it would work... and about the money. Christ's sake, fifty thousand dollars. I don't know how to handle that kind of money."

"I'm sure that you will soon learn and I will be at your disposal." The attorney smiled, "Mr. Ito advised me that the difficult part will come from your large friend, Sergeant Edwards. I understand he is a very thirsty fellow."

"Yes, he will be a problem in more ways than one. He and Sol will be looking over my shoulder every time I spend money. Thank you... I'll call you after I read these instructions."

Montez walked out of the office in a daze and headed for Mariko's house. What will happen if Shelby dies and I'm gone? Mr. Ito appeared to take it all in stride—Americans were rich and had lawyers to take care of their affairs. Montez knew he took his duty as Mariko's protector seriously, especially if Shelby died.

Sol and Edwards anxiously waited for them. An ashtray full of cigarette butts sat on the table.

"Well, don't just stand there looking ugly; talk to us," Edwards blurted, as Montez walked in.

"First, were you able to see Shelby?" Montez asked.

"No change," Sol answered. "He hasn't come out of the coma, and they wouldn't let us see him."

Montez detailed his meeting with the attorney without mentioning the money. That was saved for a savory moment.

"When is Mariko coming home?" Sol asked. "We've been waiting for information long enough."

Montez turned to Mr. Ito, "You told us she was fine; we know she's financially secure. Now we need to know when she's coming home."

Mr. Ito walked deliberately around the room making barely audible sucking sounds. "Mariko home very soon. Kanji and Takie bring her home — she stay safe with them. You no scare her with talk. She believes Shelby-san soon be okay. Mariko believe GI doctor fix everything. She know big specialist doctor come from Japan." His teacher's voice changed to one of entreaty, "You help Mariko and Shelby-san. Police find bad men who hurt Shelby-san. They not important. Wakarimaska? You understand?"

"Those APs couldn't find their ass if it wasn't attached," said Edwards in disgust. "We know who did this and we're going to get 'em."

Mr. Ito sighed, "Montez-san, talk to empty-headed one."

"I hate to say this, but Edwards speaks our mind," interjected Sol. "However, our first step is to see that Mariko and Shelby are safe and taken care of in the future. I think we can...."

A pedicab drew up to the walkway and a very pregnant Mariko slowly stepped out. Her face broke into a big smile, "I'm so happy I cry to see you, Montez-san, Edwards-san, Sol-san. I think of you everyday and I very lonely."

Edwards swooped on her. "Easy boy," said Montez, "You want to crush her and the baby?"

Edwards stopped his advance and gently hugged her. Montez turned to Takie and Kanji. "We'd like to thank you for taking care of Mariko. I know it must have cost a lot, so we'll pay for everything."

The two young men glanced at Mr. Ito, bowed and melted out the door.

"Damn!" exclaimed Montez. "I just insulted them. Mr. Ito, will you apologize for me."

"Nevertheless, those boys can't afford it," Sol insisted. "We can find some way to pay them."

"I know," said Montez. "Mr. Ito, ask them if they will act as body guards for Mariko. Tell them they will be well paid for lost work. I'm sure they'll accept that from you."

"They good boys and return soon... no sweat, Montez-san," said Mariko. "I need fix house and make soba just like before."

Mariko wandered through the house, touching a small table, then a chair. Although all vestiges of the attack were gone, Montez saw her eyes well with tears before she turned her face to hide her emotion.

"I know Shelby-san will be home soon. You ask doctors so I can visit Shelby-san." Mariko scampered to the kitchen to prepare the soba and rice cakes.

"Mariko, what happened when those men

broke into your house?"

"We hear noise outside, then near door. Shelby-san know noise bad and tell me to run to trees and then to Mr. Ito's house. I ran fast... scared, to Mr. Ito. I hide behind trees, hear fight noise in house. I wake Mr. Ito and he go see Shelby-san. He tell me to stay in house. After, Mr. Ito not let me see Shelby-san."

"Did you see anyone break in? Sol asked. "I mean, did you see or hear the bad GIs talk?"

"Iie... no, Sol-san. I only hear hard noises in house. I know Shelby-san have big trouble. I no can help him. I have baby in stomach."

"We've got as much information as we're going to get from her and Mr. Ito," Sol said to his friends, then jumped abruptly to his feet. "Hell, we know who did it. Let's find them and kick their asses."

Silence met his outburst.

"Well, you're not the only ones that want to see justice done," Sol said sheepishly. "However, I suppose we do need some evidence before we kick ass."

"I'll be goddamned," said Edwards. And they all laughed.

Montez looked at the small group and smiled; the somber house had awakened. Shelby's fight for life made him realize that getting Easley was a minor issue. He had to ensure that Mariko and the baby were taken care of in case Shelby was incapacitated for an extended time... or if he died.

Montez figured he would be rotated state-side in March or April, 1953 — he had two or three months to complete his obligation. Edwards would finish his tour of duty even earlier.

The air war was winding down again. The normal post-mission maintenance time of two or three days on B-29s was relaxed. Montez knew that his old war bird had flown WWII missions over Japan and needed extensive maintenance; however, the "Pesky Fly" would most likely be flown stateside and scrapped. Or mothballed. There was no gratitude for past performance when the pall of obsolescence descended on fatigued metal or old soldiers.

They arrived late at the base and trekked to the hospital to see Shelby. Allowed to peek in Shelby's room, they saw a tube in his nose, another in his mouth, and another tube connected to a clear plastic bag, coiled under the white sheet, and probably to his arm. A folded blue blanket lay on the foot of his bed. The ten by fifteen-foot white room had a three-inch blue line at bed level on all the walls, a metal table with medical equipment, tape, and bottles partially filled with fluid. The austere room also had a monitoring device with wires hooked up to Shelby.

The night nurse, with a blonde mustache and facial hair, came to his room. She clucked like a mother hen as she shooed them out of the room. "His wounds are healing nicely," she said.

"Have you any further information from the

specialist? His regular doctor told us two days ago that there was nothing new to report."

"I'm sorry," the nurse replied, "There is no change. You should talk to his doctor for further information."

"I don't know what to tell Mariko," said Montez as they walked out of the dark hospital. "She wants to see him, but the hospital says no."

"Monty, I've been thinking about it and maybe you're right," said Edwards as they trudged to the barracks. "We got to think of Mariko and beat the hell out of Easley at our leisure."

"That's my job," answered Montez. "You promised. And besides you can beat everybody else's ass all by your lonesome."

"Well, goddamn it, I get one too," said Sol, with a grimace.

"I'll save you one," Edwards answered.

They slowed their pace to admire the lazy moon crowning the darkening hills, just in time to give light to the airmen working on their aircraft. They were interrupted by their crewmember, Lindstrom.

"Where in the hell do you guys go to? We're scheduled tomorrow at 0400. The Fly's going to carry 500-pound bombs and a full gas load. It's apparently a long mission."

The next morning Montez arrived at the hardstand early. The aircraft's ground crew began to dribble in before 0400, along with some armament and other specialists. Lindstrom was topping off the 7000-gallon fuel tanks. The crew chief, Sergeant Pappas, was running checks on a troublesome number two engine. Montez watched the armament people finish loading 500-hundred-pound General Personnel bombs. Each bomb was fitted with a delayed-action fuse consisting of a propeller on the bomb's nose.

The bombs were timed to detonate in from 1 to 144 hours. Because these bombs could be de-fused by the Chinese, a groove was milled into the main body of the fuse. Any attempt to re-move the fuse triggered the bomb's explosion. The external casing of the GP bomb was scored so when the bomb exploded, shrapnel would shower the area near the blast.

The aircrew arrived in a six by six truck; offi-cers, including the aircraft commander, jumped off a following jeep. The aircrew kicked tires, ex-amined wings, guns, propellers, and fuselage. They never found anything amiss, observed Montez, with a sense of pride. Even so, he hated being an aircraft mechanic. On the other hand, he was grateful for not being sent to B-29 gun-nery school and getting his ass shot off. One of his classmates at A&E school graduated when he did, but was assigned to fighters in Korea. He was killed when the forward airbase he was as-signed to was overrun by the North Koreans. When it was your turn, it was your turn.

The flight crew lined up for inspection by the aircraft commander. Their equipment—side arms, parachutes, earphones, flight helmets, and other gear needed for the mission — was stacked neatly behind them. The commander slowly moved down the line of airmen, inspecting each piece of equipment to see if it was combat ready. When finished, he ordered the crew to don their parachutes and Mae West life jackets and begin loading their equipment into the bomber.

Montez realized that he might not see this again and he watched the flight crew's procedure with renewed interest. When the crew was in the aircraft, he walked over to a large fire extinguisher, pushed it close to engine number three, and waited for the crew to finish its preflight check. Soon, the signal to start the engine was given. The propeller reluctantly turned, the engine whined, coughed, then roared to life — like a slap on a newborn's behind evoking an angry cry. Soon, all four engines were roaring and the signal to pull the chocks from the huge wheels freed the bomber from its earthly tether.

The B-29 rumbled from the hardstand to position itself on the runway. Montez visualized the pilot setting the plane's brakes before he ran the engines to full power. The aircraft vibrated in anticipation until the brakes were released, and takeoff power on the four screaming engines pulled the heavy bomber down the runway and off to the target with its airborne brothers.

When quiet descended on the hardstand, Montez turned to Edwards. "We don't have many missions left. I heard Jimmy ask the commander if this was one of their last missions. The Commander just smiled at him."

Edwards wasn't listening. He was staring hard at Sergeant Easley.

"Easy boy." Montez warned Edwards, then gazed, transfixed, at the sun, which blushed on the horizon. He always felt alone at this time, drinking in the beauty of the ascending orange-red sun on the mountain peaks. With difficulty, Montez snapped out of his trance and trotted to a waiting truck.

"We need a plan on how to deal with Easley," whispered Montez, so that others on the short truck ride to the barracks wouldn't hear. "All we've talked about is beating him up. What we do depends on Shelby. If he pulls through, I'll beat the hell out of Easley. But what if…you know, he doesn't make it?"

"We'll kill the bastard!" Edwards roared, bringing the sleepy crew members to attention. Montez glared at him. When nothing else was said, the men lost interest. They shifted on the wood bench seats — an unattainable search for a comfortable position.

They jumped off the truck in front of the barracks. "Okay. Now we can talk," said Montez. "Let's find Sol and figure this out, once and for all."

They caught up to Sol on his way to the mess hall. "Let's talk while we get some chow. You guys look like you've been up for some time."

"Some of us must do heroic deeds for our

country," Edwards replied. "The world will thank us someday."

"Christ almighty," exclaimed Montez," don't get him going or we'll never get down to business."

Waiting in the long line of sleepy men in the steamy mess hall, Montez began a quiet discussion on what should be done. "Basically, we need to stay low until Shelby pulls out of it. If…when he comes out of the coma, he may be able to tell the APs who did it." Montez added with reluctance, "If Shelby doesn't make it, then we have a real problem. We're talking about murder and the police have to handle it…with our help, whether they want it or not."

They grabbed dinged metal trays from a large stack. Each got three pieces of white bread and smothered them with chipped beef in cream sauce, vulgarly known to every GI as "shit on the shingle." Very few asked for the runny, half-done powdered eggs or the wet grey lumps the cooks called oatmeal. Near the end of the line, they smelled cinnamon rolls — they were early enough to find some left.

Sol poured coffee from a large metal container. "You guys must've been thinking this over for some time. If Shelby doesn't make it, the police have to take care of it — it's murder. We should look for evidence to help them tie in Easley." He gingerly sipped the hot coffee. "But you know, I don't trust the APs. Besides not being too bright, they're not taking this as seriously as they should."

"Well, I guess we agree on what we're gonna do," said Edwards. "I know ol' Shelby will make it—he's too damn ugly and rich to die."

They all muttered assent. Mariko's future was discussed again until there was nothing else to say. After two cups of strong black coffee, Sol headed for the Operations shack for a long workday. Montez and Edwards, in greasy fatigue coveralls, trudged to the hospital to see Shelby. Later they would change into their khakis and visit Mariko.

The doctor was in the hospital, but he was a hard man to find. They waited until he walked out to the main hallway. Montez approached him. "We haven't had a chance to talk to you in over a week, Doc. Has anything changed?"

"There's no real change," replied the doctor. "His wounds are healing nicely; however, his eye will remain bandaged, as will his ribs for a while longer. I can't tell you anything else about the coma. We can't do anything more at this time. He may be lucid at any time or it may go on for an indeterminate period, or worse. All in all, he's doing well considering the severe beating. The ophthalmologist said his eye should be fine."

"What do you mean, or worse? Montez asked.

"He may never come out of it."

"Can his wife see him?"

"I'm sorry. Our records show she is not his

wife. I understand his attorney is trying to fix all that, but it's not legal yet." The doctor raised his hands to stop the expected rebuttals. He'd been through it before. "I tell you what, let me work on some kind of pass for her; but I'm not promising anything."

They thanked him and walked to Shelby's room.

"He looks good, don't you think?" Edwards asked. "The doc seems optimistic about the coma."

Montez stared at the tubes in his arms and the wires leading to a monitor. Shelby's zits and pockmarked skin seemed oddly clear and smooth. "His face seems to be nearly healed," said Montez gruffly, to hide the tremor in his voice. "We can't do any good here." After a couple of minutes, they hurried out of the hospital.

"Let's clean up and see Mariko," Montez said. "She needs to be brought up to date...but let's not tell her everything."

The airmen were silent in the bouncing pedicab, each deep in thought. The usual banter and comments about the Okinawans they saw on the road, especially pretty girls, wa missing.

"I believe I've done just about all I can with the lawyers," said Montez abruptly. "I called the lawyer in Boston, Mr. Day, and he said I worry too much. I told him I was going stateside in two or three months. I said you were too. Don't worry, he said."

"Those ol' legal boys ain't pregnant or had

the crap beat out them by some bastards. Well, you know what I mean."

Montez grinned, "I know what you mean. I hope you go to school with me in California to learn English so the world can understand you. Don't forget, I've nearly finished a college semester through those USAFI courses you make fun of. I'm one of the few educated people that can understand you."

"Boy, you still don't talk good American like me. Anyhow, I'm going to be in college before you even get back home. I'll teach you American when you get home. You'll need it in God's country."

They pulled up to the small village and saw Mariko was well guarded. The two Okinawan martial art students and Mr. Ito hovered outside her house.

"Mr. Ito, how is everything?" Montez bowed formally to his teacher.

"Hokay, Montez-san. Mariko worry about Shelby-san. APs find bad GIs?"

"They're too dumb to find anything," Edwards interrupted. "But we'll take care of them."

Mr. Ito stared at Edwards with his usual look of wonderment. "Does tall bacatare one say truth?"

"Edwards-san is a lout and, yes, crazy — but he means well. However, he is probably close to the truth about the police."

Mariko heard the commotion and rushed clumsily to embrace her friends. "You see

Shelby-san? He hokay now?"

"We saw him a little while ago and he…he looks much better. Doctors take good care of him." Montez led her back into the house. "But we have to talk about you and the baby. You too, Mr. Ito, please. We have to talk."

Chapter 14

Discussion

The small group sat around a low, gleaming mahogany table sipping aromatic hot tea. Edwards, as usual, sat at the corner of the table, long skinny legs uncomfortably straddling each side.

"Mariko, please sit down," Montez said, tugging at her elbow. "Leave the rice cakes until we finish talking."

She reluctantly perched on a chair like an alarmed bird ready to take flight. "I feel better you talk. I bring food…."

"No, you must listen… hard," insisted Montez. "We talked to the lawyers who will have money for you all the time. Mr. Ito has the names and knows what you should do. When Shelby-san comes home, he can take care of money, but now you must take care of it. I will help you. You must also learn to do things yourself in case Shelby-san doesn't come home." Montez quickly added, "I mean just in case he doesn't, but we feel that he will be okay. Mr. Ito will take care of you until he comes home from the hospital. If anything goes wrong or you have any questions, you talk to Sol. So, don't you worry. Wakarimaska, you understand?"

She nodded, a somber look on her plain round face. "Wakarimasu, Monty-san. I understand... arigato gozaimas." Mariko stood up, smoothed her brown knee-length kimono over her protruding stomach, and bowed her head briefly. "Thank you velly much... all of you, and what you do for me."

Edwards disentangled himself from the table, "We go stateside pretty soon. You got a lot to learn, like take care of a baby and stay away from bad GIs... and, well, you know."

"No sweat," answered Mariko breezily. "I take care of everything. When Shelby-san come home, all be bettah."

They sipped their tea in silence while Mariko served the rice cakes. There was nothing else to be said about her future. Everything from the Okinawan doctor who would deliver the baby to the color of baby clothes had been discussed and prepared for. Montez believed he could go home in peace. Yet, he didn't feel happy. His friends couldn't talk about anything except going back to "the real world."

Montez and Edwards left early to return to the base.

"Why don't we stop at New Koza for a beer?" Montez said, as they neared a well-lit village in their pedicab. "Now I don't feel like going to the base."

"Now you're talking, boy. Maybe we can find some pretty musumes. First, we have to talk a bit. I was going to tell you when we got back to the base, but its better this way."

New Koza, a village near Kadena Air Force Base, was jumping. Every house and bar was full of drinking servicemen, one arm around a girl, the other hand clasping a large Nippon beer. A couple of drunken soldiers bumped into Edwards as they walked down the dusty main drag looking for a place to sit and talk.

"Hey, buddy," one growled. "Watch your goddamned ass."

His friend looked groggily at Edwards towering over them. "Why don't you pick on someone your own size?" he muttered, as he pulled his belligerent companion away.

Montez noted that Edwards didn't even look at them. He had a thoughtful look on his face—not at all like him. Montez saw four airmen vacate a table, and he scrambled through a knot of airmen and musumes to claim the space. The light-brown clapboard walls of the small, crowded restaurant were full of the ubiquitous colorful Japanese calendars showing pretty smiling girls drinking Cokes. The vacant, scarred wood table boasted a dirty bottle of soy sauce and a sticky jar of chili oil on an inexplicably clean white dish. The noise level was deafening; but Montez liked the song, Tokyo Boogie Woogie, playing on a tinny record player older than he was. The combined odor of beer, food, perfume and armpits made for a powerful bouquet.

Edwards scooted into a too-small chair. "Jesus H. Christ! I guess it's always been like this, but this place is smellier than a constipated polecat full of ex-lax."

"I don't think so. I've never seen so many guys here. Maybe it's because the war's slowing down and they have more time off. Anyway, we'll get used to it."

After a long swallow of beer, Edwards looked at Montez. "I was going to tell you about this at the base, but this is better. I know who the guys are who beat up Shelby." Edwards moved closer to Montez. "You're not going to like this—one was ol' Whitey, the other Foley. You probably don't know Foley; he's an idiot, but Whitey went with us during the monsoon."

"Goddamn it! Not Whitey. Hell, I know him. He's not the type to do something like that. Are you sure? I know he's a hothead and gets into fights, but it's usually when he's pushed."

"Monty, I'm sure. I was drinking with a bunch of ol' boys at the NCO club. It fell in my lap without even trying. That idiot Foley started bragging about how he and Whitey beat the shit out of some ugly bastard married to a gook. He described the location perfectly." Edwards paused for a moment. "The asshole thought it was funny. I nearly stomped him right then and there, but I needed to know if Easley was involved."

Edwards viciously smashed a cigarette in the ashtray and reached for another.

"Well, did he mention him?" Montez prodded.

"Not by name. But he said the Sarge kept Whitey from killing him. It could only have been Easley. When I asked a question, Foley clammed up. I hope he was drunk enough to forget I was there."

"OK, now we know there were three of them," said Montez in a quiet voice. "It was Easley—I know it. Whitey and Foley were out for some fun, and Easley got them into this. They're yours. I don't care what you do to them."

"As soon as Shelby gets well and lets us know the story, I'm going to have some fun with those good ol' boys," said Edwards.

A thin smile crossed Montez's face, "I don't know if I'm going to have fun with Easley, but he'll wish he hadn't gone out that night."

They sat quietly drinking their beer until they heard angry drunken voices and breaking glass—a brawl. They just looked at each other.

"We're getting old, boy," said Edwards shaking his head. "Weren't too long ago we'd be the first there to see the action."

"I guess so. I've been thinking…."

"Bad move, Monty. Don't do any thinking; it'll only get you in trouble."

"Look, you dumb redneck; we got just a couple months to go. I know we've talked about it before, but we were usually bombed." Montez waited for a moment to focus Edwards' attention. "Are you really going back to Tennessee or are you going to school in California?"

Edwards fidgeted with his beer. "I have to go back home to see the folks. I have a lot of things to do...to correct. What I don't know is how long I'm going to stay there or if I'm even leaving. One thing I do know — I'm going to school."

"Well, at least you're doing something right." Montez grinned at the thoughtful face. "I was hoping you'd go to school in California so I could help you. You need all the help you can get, you know. And don't forget, Sol will be there if I'm not around to show you the ropes."

"I tell you, boy, I'm an A-student all the way. You'll be lucky if you get into college."

"Take it easy, Sonny," interjected Montez. "I just wanted to know if you're thinking about it...apparently you are. Your folks aren't going to recognize you in them thar hills with shoes."

Edwards opened his mouth, but Montez beat him to it. "Have you decided what you're going to major in — what you want to do?"

"I don't know. I'll make up my mind after I'm home for a while. What about you?"

"I'm thinking of a business degree. Then maybe law school." Montez' gaze swept the restaurant where GIs chug-a-lugged their beer and haggled with the prostitutes over prices. All at once, the grungy picture began to take on the irrational clarity of a dream: flattened drone of music, voices. "Never hoppen, GI. Two dollah, one timo. Me good stuff."

Then the hustling and cursing faded. Montez felt his body pull back, rise out of his chair, then above the scene. He saw himself and everyone else, but there was only the faint hum of sound and no smell. Never had he felt so happy, so free from cares.

He felt he was leaving, floating away. The crowd was growing smaller and then something told him he had to stop. He wanted to stay up there, to just float joyfully for a while longer, but he was afraid he wouldn't be able to return. He willed himself to descend and the room started to come towards him.

He found himself sitting idly at the table holding his beer bottle in his hand as if nothing had happened. He was quiet for a while, wondering what had occurred. He glanced at Edwards to see if he'd noticed anything.

Edwards was busy looking at the girls and making comments about their attributes.

Montez wanted to get out of the place and think. "Let's head back to the base. Maybe they'll let us see how ol' Shel is doing."

Reluctantly, Edwards stood up. "Boy, you sure know how to stop a fellow from having a little fun." He had been eyeing a pretty, bosomy girl on a GI's lap.

He disentangled himself from the small table and chairs. "First, you say let's have some fun, then you start bitching about having some."

"I just saved your redneck from getting bro-ken," said Montez. To hide his confusion, he kept up the banter. "I don't even get a thank you for taking care of you, making sure you're fed, get-ting your diaper changed...."

He shook his head in mock sadness.

Chapter 15

Tracking

It was dusk when they arrived at the quiet hospital. Sol looked up as they came in and quickly walked to them. "Shelby's dead. He died two hours ago...never came out of the coma."

"Goddamn it...damn it!" exclaimed Edwards. "What happened? He seemed to be doing so great."

"They don't really know," replied Sol. "I came over about an hour after dinner; and I noticed a lot of action in his room, but the nurse wouldn't tell me what was happening. I waited until the doctor came out. He said he never came out of the coma. They tried everything, he said. He was never in pain."

Montez sat down, vaguely hearing Sol and Edwards talking about how to tell Mariko. He finally looked up at the now quiet men and found them looking at him.

"We have to tell Mariko and Mr. Ito," said

Edwards. "Then we have to find Easley and.... "

"This is not the time to think about Easley," cut in Sol. "We have to plan our course of action. After we see Mariko, we talk to the APs and see what they're going to do. This is murder. They have to treat it seriously." Sol looked at his hands for a moment. "I think I should deal with the police from this moment on. You guys are leaving soon, and I need to follow through to insure the APs do their job after you leave."

"You're right," said Montez. "But let's not tell Mariko tonight. It's late. We better hit the sack and try to get some sleep. Ed, we have to talk to the crew chief and see if we're due on the flight line tomorrow."

They walked back to their barracks deep in their own thoughts. The soft, starry night allowed a brief stream of light trailing a falling star. Montez could see his companion's faces lit by the unclouded bright Okinawan moon.

"I'm going to kill that bastard," Montez's voice sounded savage to himself. "I going to follow him every free minute I have until I can get him alone on the base or in the village. But I'm going to kill the son-of-a-bitch."

"Don't start going crazy on us, Monty," said Sol as he peered into Montez's face. "We need everyone to be on board when we talk to the APs. And I mean thinking straight—not going on a kamikaze mission."

"Look son," joined Edwards trying to lighten the mood. "I'm going to beat the shit out Whitey and Foley. Let's not talk crazy about killing."

"Don't forget I get one of them," added Sol.

"I don't care what you guys do," said Montez quietly. "I'm going to get him the same way he killed Shelby. Don't worry…it will be planned and I'm going to take my time. Shelby was my friend and I promised him I would take care of things. I'll be on board with everything else, all the way."

Edwards put his hand on Monte's shoulder. "Don't worry, they'll pay."

Reaching their barracks, they checked the duty log and found they were on next morning. Sol had to deliver the news to Mariko by himself. Heads bowed, they separated and walked to their barracks.

Next morning, the crew chief was pulling equipment into place to work on number four engine. An engine check had indicated a faulty magneto. Montez wondered if the chief got there early to impress the crew, then decided differently. He loved his plane. It belonged to him.

Pulling the engine nacelle cowling while he stood on the tall work platform, Montez studied Sergeant Easley. He looked relaxed and happy as he joked with one of the crew members. No worry in the world. Good, Montez thought, that would make it easier to track him on and off the base until he could predict his movements.

Montez gauged Easley's strength and quickness, remembering Edwards warning not to underestimate him. Easley outweighed him by at least forty pounds and though slightly shorter, with a fat belly, he had huge shoulders, arms and hands. Doesn't matter, he thought. Surprise and speed were on his side. He jumped when Edwards shook the platform.

"Wake up, boy. You're supposed to be working, not goldbricking."

He knew Edwards understood what he was up to. Edwards clambered up the rungs to help him remove the old magneto. He stuck his long arms in the nacelle opening.

"Boy, you be careful now. I see how you keep looking at him — like a fox figuring out a way into the chicken coop."

"Ed, don't worry about it. I'm going to take care of things the right way."

The "Pesky Fly" would need extensive work, but there was no hurry finishing the job. With the war winding down, they wouldn't be working at night. Edwards, Moretti, Ericson and the rest of the ground crew talked about how they were going to spend their evenings and guessed when the old war bird would be flown home. It would be easy to track Easley every night. The problem would be getting away from Edwards, but he'd find a way.

While on top of the wing, Montez saw the last B-29 in the group take off for Korea, sun glinting off the aircraft's silver body. The plane lifted off the runway; then he saw the right wing slowly, majestically, dip toward the earth and the aircraft disappeared from view.

A thunderous explosion followed by a violent force thrust Montez into the plane's fuselage. Shaken, he came down one platform while the clamorous ground crew went up another platform's rungs to see what happened. After he answered questions as well as he could, they tried to figure out for over an hour what caused the plane to crash. The crew chief, chewing his usual cigar stump, yelled for them to get back to work. It suddenly struck him as never before how important his work was. Could the crash be due to a ground crew member's mistake? How many times had he taken a short cut, nothing serious — he would have flown in the plane, yet who knows? He'd never do that again.

Then he thought about the crew — after all those missions over Korea, the entire crew gone in a second. He was glad he didn't know the airmen in that aircraft.

After work, Edwards jumped on a truck with some of the ground crew and waved at him to hurry.

"I'll meet you at the mess hall, Ed." Montez said. A plan half formed in his mind.

He went directly to his room, showered quickly, dressed, and walked to Easley's barracks. Montez spotted some tall brush a short distance from the entrance — a good place to watch the barracks and the street.

Half an hour later, Easley ambled out with a staff sergeant and headed for the main gate. Montez figured that if Easley got a ride outside the gate, he could intercept him. There were always pedicabs outside of the gate.

Easley and his buddy were already in a cab when Montez reached the gate, breathing heavily, his khaki blouse wet and sticky. There were no pedicabs. Too many airmen on leave with the war winding down, Montez thought. He started an easy lope down the dusty road, hoping to keep the cab in sight. He ran over a mile, passing astonished Okinawans, until he found a pedicab. He jumped in while it was still moving and yelled to the driver, "Keep that cab in sight!" The wide-eyed driver looked at him.

"You got money, boss?"

"I got beaucoup money," said Montez, digging into his pocket and pulling out a handful of scrip. "See? Mucho dinero, comprende, muchacho?" Montez liked to speak Spanish to the Okinawans. It helped dealing with them, especially the men. He felt it made him different from the conquering soldiers.

"Isoginasai! You hurry, catch cab pronto, but not too close."

"Hokay. No sweat. Hey boss, you Mexico boy?"

"Hai, me ichiban Mexico boy. Wakarimaska? You understand? I'm the best ichiban Mexico boy in Okinawa. You just catch that cab."

The driver turned to Montez and said, with a huge smile. "No sweat. Me ichiban best hot-damned Okinawa boy. I take care and catch GI."

"What's your name?"

"Everybody call me Joe, boss."

"Okay, your name is Jose in Spanish. My name is Juan."

The driver grinned at his new name and looked quizzically at Montez. "You going to beat shit out of that GI, boss?"

"Name is Juan. Right now I only want to know where he goes."

"Hokay, boss... Juan. I take you, we find GI pretty soon."

Twenty minutes later, Easley's cab turned off on a two-lane hard-packed dirt road and passed two small villages. At a third larger village set in a hilly area covered with small pine trees and high grass, Easley walked to a house set back from the road, slid open the thin slat and paper door and strolled in without knocking. His staff sergeant buddy continued walking until he reached a different house, where he knocked on the door. After a few words, he went inside.

The village was like many others throughout the island — dusty shacks clustered along the main road running through town, with brush and other houses scattered loosely around them. Montez sat in the cab studying the house and the surrounding area. The clapboard house backed up to a grove of dwarf pine trees partially obscuring a trail leading to an outhouse. The house was surrounded by heavy brush. High grassy knolls hid the house from its neighbors. He saw a small restaurant down the road.

"Jose, let's go to the restaurant, get some

soba. You like soba?"

"Yes sir. I eat soba all time."

Montez stepped from the cab and headed for the restaurant until he noticed that his driver was still sitting on his dilapidated once-red bicycle.

"Hayaku, Jose. I'm hungry."

"Don't know, Juan-boss. Maybe you get soba."

"Whatsa matter, you chicken shit? No eat with amigo?"

"Me no chicken shit... maybe not good, eat with boss."

"My name is Juan, not boss. Do you think it's not good to eat with GI?"

Montez waited for an answer, although he knew young Okinawans men didn't mix with GIs. He saw Jose's face reflect his decision to go into the small restaurant with him. He jumped off his seat and followed him into the two-table restaurant, where Montez moved a small table close to a window to see the road fronting Easley's house. An older woman wearing a plain brown kimono with a large red sash minced over in white socks and new getas. She looked at the Okinawan driver curiously, then bowed.

"Konbanwa, Mamasan. Please bring soba and maybe two birus. Jose anything else you want?"

Jose intently studied the dog-eared pale blue menu and finally looked at Montez. "Maybe no soba." He pointed to a picture of a hamburger.

"Maybe hamburger and Coke." He glanced at the mamasan, then at Montez. His driver couldn't read English, Montez realized.

"Maybe I want french fries." Jose casually said as he put down the menu.

"Okay. Mamasan bring two sobas, Cokes, and two hamburgers. And french fries for my friend."

Montez reached over to the window and pushed aside the old yellow lace curtains. Now he had a clear view of the road. He would stay until dark. Montez noted that Jose was studying him as he looked out the window.

"You kick ass of bad sergeant pretty soon? He pretty big sergeant."

"Well, he's a piss-poor sergeant. He need takusan ass-kicking, but maybe later."

Prying his eyes from the road, he looked at Jose. He appeared to be about eighteen years old, small, with a slight, muscular body and quick observant eyes. His head was topped with a shock of black hair and his brown face easily broke into a broad grin.

"You're pretty smart, Jose. Do you want to help me keep track of the sergeant? I'll pay you."

"Sure, Juan-boss. I look for you and no-good sergeant all time. I'm ichiban boy in everything."

It's a deal then. How will you know when the sergeant leaves the base?"

No sweat. I have friends. They tell me," Jose smiled broadly. "I know everything that happen—many friends in Okinawa have cab."

Montez realized he had just hired the best detective service on the island. He also recognized that it could be dangerous, all of Jose's friends knowing his business.

"Jose, don't tell anyone why I want to follow sergeant. Okay? This will be secret between us."

"No sweat. I don't tell anyone. Anyway, friends don't care about GIs. I know many things about GIs." He winked, then added, "I know GI that killed Negro GI. I know where he hide gun — we got gun."

"Christ's sake!" Montez said and looked at his driver to see if he was bragging. He wasn't.

They talked for an hour until sunset. Montez found Jose fascinating, comical, and a fount of information. He knew when the planes were flying missions the next day and when they were due back — the Okinawan girls working at the base overheard everything. He knew the news of the island before it was reported to anyone, even Armed Forces Radio, including who was doing what to whom in the indigenous community.

"Even mamasan have good time sometime. Not with GI and sometime not with papasan." A huge grin transformed Jose's face, revealing brilliant white teeth with two large gold teeth prominently displayed in front. "Maybe someone else with mamasan, wakarimaska? You understand?"

"You're a devil. I can see that." Montez smiled and punched him in the shoulder.

"I write to my cousin in Brazil. Tell him what

happen. Meet Mexico boy and have new Spanish name and kick ass of bad sergeant."

"They speak Portuguese in Brazil, not Spanish, you know. Beside you're supposed to keep this quiet."

"No sweat. I write Okinawa language. He too far. No tell anyone."

Montez decided he couldn't do anymore here and told Jose to take him to Mariko's village. He could see the questions in his eyes. He must know of Mariko and Shelby, the beating, but not of Shelby's death. He decided to confide in him — he would know eventually.

Montez's mind was as bumpy as the ride, knowing what Mariko must be going through. Halfway to the village, he decided not to tell her of his plans for Easley. But he would let her know about using Shelby's money to help bring Easley to justice. Shelby would have approved.

His mind was too focused on Easley, he acknowledged. He had to call the attorneys and write a letter to Shelby's parents. Shelby had confided that his parents were in a state of shock due to his marriage to an Okinawan and her pregnancy. Shelby found it ironic that the only time they cared about him was when he found happiness. They didn't know she had been a prostitute. They would never know.

A few blocks from the village, Montez related Shelby and Mariko's story, including Shelby's death.

"I know, Juan-boss. Everybody know what

happened to GI and Okinawa girl. Very sad." Suddenly his face changed. "Not you worry. I find bad sergeant all the time. He go nowhere I don't know."

"Okay, I want you to be at the gate every evening. If I'm not there by 1830 hours, by 6:30, you can leave. I'll pay you for all your time," Montez added. "We follow sergeant every night until we know what he does."

"No sweat. I follow him if you no can go. I tell you."

They reached Mariko's house. "I wait for you, Juan-boss. You need ride to base."

"I don't know how long I'll be here."

"No sweat. I wait."

Mariko met him at the door, her arms outstretched. Mr. Ito stood behind her, then a red-faced Edwards. Mariko cried and briefly clung to Montez.

"I'm so sorry, Mariko. He died peacefully, like if he was sleeping," he said as they moved into the house.

"Where in the hell you been? Christ's sake, everybody's been worried 'bout you. Do that again and I'll kick your ass." Edwards paced up and down the immaculate front room. "Easley and his boys could have killed you. He doesn't like greaslies."

"He calls us greasers, not greaslies."

"Well, anyway, just don't do it again."

"Take it easy, Ed. Easley doesn't know I'm after him. Anyway, I can take care of myself."

Mr. Ito, calm as usual, looked at Edwards as if he were a child having a tantrum. "Perhaps we have tea now," he said and nodded to Mariko.

She arranged the cakes on the polished table and ceremoniously poured tea for the now quiet group. Mariko gave Montez a weak smile. Her face was pale with dark circles under her eyes. She was enormous, he thought. She could have the baby any moment.

Montez told the seated group about his new helper. "He's waiting for me outside. He's a nice kid, so maybe we should invite him in?" He looked at Mr. Ito who nodded his head.

Jose took to the group immediately, although Mr. Ito continued to study the Okinawan boy. Jose kept glancing at Edwards, especially when he repositioned his long legs at the table. "Edwards-san tall even for GI."

"My magnificent body is tall, but it houses a powerful brain."

Montez wondered what Jose thought of this strange gathering.

After serving tea, Mariko got her guests' attention and softly said, "I have baby maybe five days." She waited for the news to register. "I have baby in my house with mama-san doctor."

Oh, God. Montez thought with a jolt, Shelby's gone. Mariko's alone, with a half-white baby, on an island controlled by a bigoted U.S. military — and he couldn't do anything about it.

"I'm happy — I have Shelby-san here." She patted her distended belly while tears started to come down her cheeks.

Montez glanced at Mr. Ito's stoic face, then at Edwards. His brown eyes welled with tears. Christ, why does he have to be so emotional? Montez swallowed over a hard lump in his throat.

Edwards wiped his eyes and honked his nose into a large handkerchief, "She's right. We can be happy for her. She has part of Shelby."

Mr. Ito's eyebrows flew up. Montez recalled Mr. Ito's original perception of Edwards — a buffoon.

Montez looked at Edwards as if seeing him for the first time. Edwards had changed from a happy go lucky kid that was always getting into trouble, to a serious young man. Things have turned around, he thought, Edwards was looking out for him.

"We have to go back to the base now," Montez said. "We'll see you every evening, Mariko, if we can."

As soon as the pedicab was on its way, Edwards turned to Montez. "Ol' buddy, I just got notified that I'm heading home in about two weeks. They'll fly me to Tachikawa Air Force Base in Japan and then it's a slow boat to San Francisco."

"Well, we knew it was coming," Montez replied. "But now that it's here, it doesn't seem real."

What was he going to do now, thought Montez. He couldn't visualize the time he had left without Edwards' droll stories and absurd suggestions for their next adventure. He didn't want it to end, but he knew it was over. He couldn't go back to what he was two years ago on that liberty ship, anymore than Edwards could.

"It's real, all right. You'll have about a month left after I leave, so don't get into trouble." Edwards said.

"No worry," Jose said. "I watch Juan-boss for you."

"I won't be around to take care of you, boy," Edwards warned. "Don't underestimate Easley."

Don't worry, Ed. You're getting worse than an old woman," Montez put his hand on Edwards' shoulder. "I'll just do what I have to do."

Chapter 16

Edwards

Montez's recent activities regarding Easley weighed heavily on Edwards' mind. He hadn't talked to him for more than a few minutes in the last few days. Although Edwards was only a few feet from where his friend worked on top of the shiny B-29 wing, Montez concentrated on inspecting the heavy black rubber de-icer boots on the wing's leading edge. Edwards studied him from his perch on the dirty yellow metal platform where he adjusted wiring on the uncowled engine. Easley and the other crew members were always close by making conversation about events impossible. The police investigation crawled, and Mariko was about to give birth. And Montez disappeared after he returned to the barracks each evening.

"Hey, Edwards, get your ass in gear. You all making that damn engine a hobby," Easley yelled, causing Edwards to drop a wrench in a next to impossible place between the pistons.

Cursing, he started to extract the wrench by pushing his long fingers between the pistons.

Montez had changed, he thought. Physically he had gained at least ten pounds in the two years he had known him. He was still slim, but the flesh on his long frame was now hard sinew, as if a sculptor had formed the muscles deep and long. Mr. Ito's training and discipline had paid off. No, it wasn't just that. It was Montez's constant look of expectancy, as if he was waiting for something. A "lean and hungry look," Edwards quoted to himself. He knew Montez was stalking Easley like an animal. He felt a little sorry for Easley—he sure wouldn't want to be in his shoes.

Edwards missed their casual bantering more than anything else. He could say anything to Montez and know he understood, even though he'd make some wise-ass remark. He missed the discussions on books they read. Montez never made fun of him anymore. Edwards discussed books with Sol, but it just wasn't the same. Shit, Sol wanted to be a writer. How could anyone discuss Homer or Tolstoy with a writer without his finding ten meanings, all cockeyed?

Edwards glanced at Montez and found him surreptitiously looking at Easley with narrowed hard eyes and lips pulled back thin against his teeth, like a copperhead ready to strike. Christ, he'd better forget about Whitey and Foley and follow Montez to keep him from doing something stupid. He walked to the Operations shack to discuss his new plans with Sol. The Nissan hut was cooled by a large fan pulling in air through the huge swamp cooler; he visited it as often as he could for a bit of coolness.

"You might as well forget about it," Sol advised. "You're leaving in about a month and then what? Montez is going to do what he wants to do. I noticed he's having Mr. Ito spend more time training him to control his blows to the body's vital points—he's never been interested in offense and kicking techniques before."

"Yeah," Edwards responded. "Kyushu strikes, that's what they're called. Coordinated strikes to the head and upper body. He's hitting those bags with closed fists."

"I'm not worried. Montez is well trained and can take care of himself." Sol said.

"I used to be afraid Easley would hurt Montez; now I'm worried about what Montez could do to Easley." Edwards added, "He can cause real damage; that's what he's training for. Montez has gotten pretty good according to that Okinawan kid who trains with him."

After work, they headed for the base police station. Lieutenant Connors grimaced, eyes rolling upward, when Sol walked in.

"There is nothing new, Sergeant Shapiro," the lieutenant snapped, his neck red with restrained anger. "I told you I'd notify you if anything came up. I'll tell you for the last time—no physical evidence, no witnesses, and no reason to interrogate anyone. I can't say it clearer than that."

"Thank you, lieutenant." Sol answered evenly. "I'll also keep you informed of our investigation."

On their way out of the station, Edwards sauntered up to the tall AP corporal he nicknamed "Skull." "You fellas sure do know how to smell things out." Apparently Skull didn't know if this was an insult, so he gave Edwards his police stare—he was good at that. "Even ma hound dog couldn't smell like that."

Sol pulled him out of the station, "Are you crazy?" Sol glanced back at the door. "We have to work with those guys."

"Let's go talk to Monty." Edwards lengthened his stride. "Then let's see Mariko." At the gate, they found Jose arguing with two airmen outside the base entrance. When the young Okinawan saw Edwards and Sol, he left the two airmen and peddled over.

"Please, you get into cab." Both men jumped in and Jose pumped hard on his bicycle pedals. "Mariko have baby! Baby boy come last night. I take Juan-boss over to see baby and he send me here."

"Well, I'll be damned!" they said simultaneously.

"How is Mariko?" Sol asked. "Is the baby okay?"

Everybody fine. Baby very nice. He cry good when hungry."

Edwards searched for a way to ask if the baby looked average—not like Shelby.

Sol chattered with Jose about Mariko and the baby until he saw Edwards' long face. "What's the matter, Ed? You look like you lost your best friend."

"I feel like a bastard," Edwards replied. "All I can think about is whether the baby looks like Shelby."

"Don't feel bad," Sol answered. "That thought went through my mind, too. All of us want to look normal, but we're all damaged in some way. Shelby on the outside, others on the inside, like John."

"Montez? What do you mean he's damaged?"

Sol sucked on his unlit pipe for a moment. "John has been told by society that he's different, culturally inferior. That he's not as smart as the Anglo kid across the street. John believed it. Then he found the Anglo kid was not so smart and he began despising them. He has an anger inside—you've seen that yourself, Ed."

"I know. We've talked about it. He ought to get away from those damned Anglos and move to Tennessee. Hell, he'd just be one of us— Scotch-Irish."

Sol smiled. "Heaven forbid. Besides, his anger may be a good thing. And when he talks about Anglos, he's speaking generically."

Edwards was troubled to hear that Monty was damaged. What the hell did damaged mean anyway? How could he be damaged when he was the one who always knew just what to do?

"Monty has changed since I first met him. I don't think he's damaged. I think he accepts those ol' Anglo people for what they are. Well, mostly," Edwards added. "I heard him discussing these problems with Mr. Ito and how meditation has changed his outlook. I believe he accepts them Anglos now, although he's gotten a little weird with all those Oriental notions."

"You got something there, Ed. But, I hope I can keep up with him." Sol added. "You know I also have some ambivalent feelings about them thar Anglos, as you say. I've also been called names because I'm a Jew."

Edwards felt better when Sol said he was a little damaged too.

"I guess I'm the only sane one left." Edwards said. "Shelby hated what his looks did to his life; people called him names and kept away from him."

"Well, if you're an example of the sane, John and I are on good terms with life."

Edwards and Sol found Mariko's house full of people. A grinning Montez came out to greet them. "The baby is great—I mean he's a pretty baby. It's hard to tell, but I think he has Shelby's grey eyes."

Edwards stepped into the house, walked to the bedroom, hugged Mariko and gently touched the baby with a long finger. All of them wanted the child to look normal, but when he looked at it, he didn't know if it was ugly or pretty—it was just a tiny blob making funny little mewing sounds.

Jose stared at the bundle from the bedroom entrance. "He have very red face and no hair." Quickly he added, "He nice baby boy."

Mariko looked at her visitors and said, "I been in bed since baby come—all night and all day. I get up now, make tea." She handed the baby to Montez before he could stop her and slowly started to sit up.

"No way," Montez said, pressing his free hand on her shoulder. "I can make tea."

"I make bettah tea, Juan-boss."

Mariko reluctantly gave up, fluffed up her pillows and accepted the baby that Montez obviously was happy to relinquish.

Montez followed Jose to the kitchen, and Edwards could hear them talking in low tones. He knew somehow that it was about Easley. Plans were being made without him and suddenly it hit him. He wasn't going to be here. He wasn't part of them anymore and felt left out. He'd waited for two years to go home and now he didn't want to leave. The book wasn't closed yet.

He moved toward Mariko. She smiled at her baby and her friends. She would probably cry after they left, sad and lonely for Shelby. He knew about loneliness. Until he met Montez, he had no real friends, had thought of himself as an oddball, a loner. Now he had friends and he was leaving them.

Edwards held her hand. "I won't forget you and little Shelby. The days and nights I spend with you and Shelby in this house was the happiest time of my life." He self-consciously stood up after a while and walked to the living room.

Later, after Edwards promised to see her every day he had off, he said goodbye to Mariko and jumped in the pedicab with Sol and Montez.

"You know, I'm sure going to miss Mariko and this place." He stared up at the starry night sky. "I think I'm even going to miss the smell, but not these tiny little pedicabs — no place to put your legs anywhere!"

"Four GI fit in my cab," their driver piped in. I have nice cushion on bench seats. My cab also convertible like car — open and close top."

"Okay, Jose. You have the best transport in all of Okinawa," Montez said. "If Edwards-san was normal size, you could fit five GIs."

With Montez and Sol captive in the cab, Edwards decided this was a good time to discuss Mariko and Easley...maybe even talk about their future in the States.

"Monty, I know you mean to really mess up Easley; but let me tell you he's not worth it, especially if you have to pay a price for it."

Montez did not reply.

"He's right, you know," Sol added. Killing that man can't help Shelby or Mariko."

Edwards played his only hand. "I told you I'm going to college in California. You said I need help, Monty; and you promised to help, so you have to be there. Sending Easley to his maker won't help me when I really need it. In fact, doing him in won't help anyone—including Shelby and Mariko."

Montez laughed at his obvious ploy; however, Edwards guessed from the look on Montez's face that he'd made a dent in his plan. Not much really, but any little bit would help.

"Ed, I'll be waiting for you in Los Angeles," Montez said. "Sol will probably be teaching or writing the great American novel, so you have no excuse to stay in God's little acre any longer than necessary."

The three men discussed their rosy California future, promising to meet in exactly one year at Sol's house in Westwood.

But through it all, Edwards couldn't get a nagging voice out of his head—an old soldier's saying that all debts and promises are forgotten when a soldier leaves.

And the look in Montez's eyes made him even more uneasy.

Chapter 17

Departure

Montez and Sol sat on a beat-up blue wooden chest at the foot of Edwards' bunk. Their eyes dull, faces grim, yet trying to be upbeat, they watched him pack a faded green duffel bag and a blue canvas suitcase. He was really leaving. Montez couldn't believe that the lanky Tennessean was not going to be around. How could someone be with you every day for two years, then be plucked away by an unseen force? It struck him how little control one had in the Air Force — you couldn't say, "Please, I want to stay a few more days." Man, he must be going crazy. No one wanted to stay any longer than he had to.

"Ed, why don't you fold your clothes instead of shoving them in? Try to be a little civilized and practice being a gentleman before you leave."

Edwards didn't reply with his usual banter. It was difficult to know what was in his mind.

He said he was happy to be going home, even excited about getting his belongings together. However, his unhappy eyes under a furrowed brow told another story.

"Well, that does it," Edwards said breezily. "I'm ready for the big time. We're going to be in Tokyo for two or three days, and I'm going to do it up."

"You're fortunate," Sol agreed. "John will be leaving right behind you, but I still have nearly six months to go."

They all knew their talk was bunk designed to mask their feelings.

"Damn!" Edwards suddenly blurted. "Both of you know how I really feel about leaving now." Edwards continued, "Not that I don't want to go home, but I'm not done here. You guys need my help with Mariko and the AP investigation. And Monty, you really need my advice on your crazy idea about Easley."

Sol stood up, pipe in hand, and pretended to look for an ashtray. He signaled Montez to back him up. "I don't know what you expect to do. I'm dealing with the police, not you. We all visit Mariko. And don't worry about Easley — that will take care of itself."

Montez kicked a dirty tee shirt toward Edwards. "Yeah, what can you do? You can't even take care of yourself. Don't worry; we're on top of it. We'll let you know how everything turns out."

"Is that a promise?" Edwards asked, suspicion in his voice. "Are you guys going to write and let me know exactly what's going on?"

"Boy Scout's honor," Sol chimed. "And I take my Scout oath seriously."

Montez chuckled. "You were never in the Boy Scouts."

"That's why I take it seriously," Sol retorted.

"All right. I give up," Edwards said. "But I'm serious now. I expect letters. Now, about how we're going to meet when we get home. I'll probably stay home for three months after I'm discharged, then head out to Californy—should be about six months."

"I'll be waiting," Montez said. "Probably be free of the Air Force two months after I get to the States. My dad moved to another town, and I have nothing there to hold me. Both my brothers are leaving soon, and one of them is joining the Marines. I couldn't talk him out of it." Montez thought for a second. "Course I remember that no one at home could talk me out of it, either. An Air Force recruiting sergeant lied like hell to get me to enlist. Anyway, L.A. is the place to be, even if Sol does live there."

Edwards' long face told Montez their friend was feeling left out. He would be in Tennessee while they would be working things out here and later in Los Angeles. "I told Mariko goodbye last night," Edwards said. "I told her if she ever needed help, I'd come back."

"She say anything?" Sol asked.

Edwards looked at the floor. "Not much.

Just…no, she didn't."

"Don't worry. Mariko and the baby are going to be just fine." Montez assured him again.

"Yeah, I know." Edwards closed the bulging blue suitcase and stood up. "The plane takes off at 0800 tomorrow, so I won't see you guys. You'll be at work, I guess."

Sol got to his feet. "I better get at least three hours sleep or I won't wake up."

Edwards put his hands in his pockets and then quickly pulled them out. After an awkward pause, he stretched his long arm to Sol to shake hands. For a fleeting moment, they felt like strangers. Montez suddenly tackled Edwards, knocking him onto his bunk. Sol piled on, pummeling them both, and the ice broke. After some scuffling, Montez pulled Edwards off the floor, put an arm around him and then shook his hand. Sol, pretending to nurse a sore shoulder, hugged Edwards and also shook his hand.

"Won't be long before we see you, Ed," Montez reassured him. "We will write and tell you everything that happens—a promise."

Quickly Sol and Montez left the room. Deep in thought, they ambled off to their barracks, where Sol sat down on the cement steps.

"You know, Ed must feel pretty bad. At least we know we'll see each other stateside. But you two knew each other before in Guam."

"Yeah. Over two years. Sure seems weird to split up."

Montez went to his room and arranged the

mosquito net around his bunk, knowing they would get in somehow and suck blood. After an hour of trying to sleep, he vaguely remembered thinking that he kept Edwards out of trouble, but lately Edwards was taking care of him.

Early next morning, Montez dejectedly walked to Sol's barracks and woke him to go to the mess hall. Perhaps they could catch Edwards before he left. He was not there. After a hurried breakfast of toast, orange juice and coffee, they caught a ride to the flight line. A C-54 was just lumbering into position for takeoff. When the plane was airborne, they trudged silently to their respective jobs.

"Hey boy, yore buddy just left." Easley smirked as Montez reached the hardstand. "Who you gonna hold hands with now?"

"Screw you, asshole!" Montez snarled.

Montez didn't care what he said to Easley now — Easley was a dead man. However, his façade had slipped; the fat sergeant was totally aware of his hatred. Easley returned to his duties without another word. Montez saw that Morelli and Lindstrom stared at him as if seeing him for the first time.

"Hey, Pisano, watch your ass," Morelli cautioned. "That bastard is mean as a constipated bull. He'll get you sooner or later."

"No problem, paisano, I can handle him."

Montez walked calmly to the small wood shack off the hardstand to get a large screwdriver. The look on Morelli's face made him chuckle.

That evening, Easley went to the same house in the quiet village, and Montez followed him. He knew he had to make his move soon—he had only two weeks before he left. His plan was simple: when Easley got to the village in the evening, Montez would get him before he stepped into the house. Easley had to be lured to the open area at the side of the house. He must not be cornered where Easley could use his superior strength. Montez was sure he had not been seen by Easley. Nevertheless, he must stop following him now that he knew his destination—Easley hadn't changed his pattern once.

His Okinawan driver noted a change in Montez as he pedaled the cab to Mariko's house. "Juan-boss, you kick ass soon?"

"Pretty soon. I don't have much time before they send me home. I think you better not be around when I go after him. You might get into trouble with the police."

"No sweat. I know Okinawa police—they my friends. You need I take care of things. I know where to go."

"Okay, okay. You can take me to do the job. It will be soon."

His driver was mollified as he took him to see Mariko and Mr. Ito. Montez didn't feel good mentally or physically until he had a strenuous session at Mr. Ito's dojo. He would visit Mariko for a while and then go to Mr. Ito's house.

Mariko seemed to know when he was coming

to visit. She greeted him outside her immaculate house; and, after a hug, she handed the baby, Shelby John Wellstone, to him. That cumbersome name was a bit too much for such a small bundle, but tonight Montez didn't joke about it. He took his shoes off and walked into the house. Montez decided to voice an idea he had been thinking about for some time.

He stopped in the main room. A long, intricately carved wooden chest gleamed from its place near a corner. "That is beautiful. Where did you get it?"

"From Mr. Ito's friend in Naha. He make nice pictures in wood. I keep all my pictures of Shelby-san, Edwards-san, Sol-san. You too. Now baby, too," She added. "Keep all presents for baby from best friends at bottom of chest."

"That's really nice, Mariko." Montez hesitated for a moment, then asked, "Have you ever thought of moving to the States? Maybe not right away." Then he added, "Think about it seriously before Junior get too old."

"I thought many times of going stateside for baby, but I'm afraid."

"Don't be afraid. I will help you and so will Sol-san and Edwards-san, even when we're far away. Then you can move to California and be with us."

Mariko looked dubiously at him, but Montez saw a glimmer of hope in her face. He would ask Sol to continue talking to her. If she showed any interest, Sol could talk to her attorney.

"I'm going to leave soon, so I want you to tell Sol-san if you want to go or if you have any questions." But Montez cautioned, "If you decide to go it may take a long time for you to get a green card to make you a legal alien."

"What is green card and rest of what you said?"

"The green card is like a passport for you to live in the States. You aren't an American citizen, but you can apply to be one later." Montez thought for a minute and added, "Because you are legally married to an American and have a baby, maybe it will be easy to leave Okinawa."

"What you say hard to understand. I think more about it."

Montez tried to convince her that Shelby Junior would be better off in the States. He didn't want to get into the problem of discrimination against Asians. Or the problems of raising a half-white child in Okinawa.

Juan listened attentively to their conversation. "I like to go States, too. Me plenty smart. Work for you in States."

"I'm sorry Jose. I would like nothing better than take you with me, but I can't even control what the Air Force does with me. I have no money, not even a job when I get back." Montez said. "But anything can happen in the future. You write to me just like Mariko, and I'll write to you."

On their way back to the base, Jose was very quiet until he suddenly exclaimed. "I have much money, nearly thousand dolla saved. You no have to take care of me."

"Christ, that's a lot of money. I'm in the wrong business. Jose, you save that money. You never know, maybe one day you can come to the States." Then Montez added, "I'll help you any way I can."

Montez said goodbye to his driver at the base gate and dragged himself towards the barracks. Right now he couldn't do much to help Mariko or Jose. Or himself.

He sucked in a lungful of the rich Okinawan air. It smelled of plowed wet earth, foliage, rotted food, and dung; and he knew he would never forget that smell.

Sol sat on the barracks cement steps. He stood up when he saw Montez and walked toward him. As he got closer, Montez saw his face in the bright moonlight. "Jesus Christ! What the hell happened to you?" He barraged him with questions until Sol raised his hand.

"I had a small altercation with Whitey a few hours ago," Sol tried to keep his battered face from smiling. "I heard him tell his buddy how he stomped a guy in the village. I guess I lost my head, called him every name in the book and asked him to meet me behind the Operations' Nissan hut. The rest is history."

"Well, I'll be damned!" He looked at Sol's face. Puffed up left eye, a nasty gash on his forehead, swollen, split lip, and a huge right cheek. "It looks like Whitey got his licks in. Come on, the rest of the story."

"Well, I did hit him good a few times, but you know, I'm not much of a fighter. Damn, it felt so good when I hit him. I was too excited to feel much pain when he hit me. Now I know what it's like to allow my latent aggressive tendencies free rein."

"Christ sakes, Sol. 'Allow latent aggressive tendencies free rein'?"

Sol smiled painfully. "Edwards was right, you know. It didn't do Whitey a bit of good to be hit, even after I called him a coward for letting three guys beat up Shelby. However, I believe it helped me some."

"Okay, Sol, I understand. You look pretty bad. Did you see a doctor?"

"A medic I know fixed me up."

"I'm going to write Ed tonight," Montez said with relish. "I'm going to tell him everything that happened to you. I'm going to make it sound like the fight of the century." He smiled at Sol, and then said, "The other night I thought of how I used to take care of that crazy scarecrow — then he changed, or I changed because of Shelby; and he started to watch over me. Strange how things are altered and you don't realize it."

Later in his bunk, Montez thought about Sol, who hated violence and had always preferred talking things out instead of fighting. Sol must have been really angry to go after Whitey that way; it wasn't normal for him. Sol wasn't the "eye for an eye" type. But neither was he. Sol said it had helped him. How? Even the score, release some anger? In a way, his confession helped Montez, too. There was right and there was wrong, justice and injustice.

About Easley, he knew he had to do what was right.

Chapter 18

Farewell

It was another perfect day in Okinawa. Montez held on tight to the slat sides of the 6X6 as it careened down the flight line of B-29s gleaming in the sun. The heat from the ball of fire rising beyond the hills made his back muscles relax. The truck suddenly slowed at the first plane, throwing his body forward; men jumped out of the truck like a production line ejecting sausages, then the truck shot forward to the next plane.

He only had four days left in Okinawa. His plane, a C-54, would leave Tuesday at 0800 hours for Tachikawa Air Force base in Tokyo; and after three days, he would be on a liberty ship to San Francisco.

All was in order: Mariko and the baby, the police, the attorneys, Mr. Ito, letters to Boston. Sol was ready to oversee the plan.

But Montez had one more chore to complete before he left — this time Sol couldn't help him.

Sol was cheerful and attached himself to Montez every moment that he was not working. "You sure are lucky. You're going to be in San Francisco at Christmas time. Of course, it's going to be windy and cold, but Christmas is a good time to be there. Any time is a good time to be there."

"You are becoming a Christian for Christmas?"

"I enjoy presents like everybody else," Sol added. "If you weren't so cheap, you'd buy me a small but expensive bauble."

Sol's buoyant attitude was a front. Mariko told him that Sol was as unhappy as she was because his friends were leaving for the States. Montez also knew Sol was glued to him, keeping track of him whenever he could. However, they didn't work together and they lived in separate barracks. Montez could ditch him easily.

Tonight would be the night. Montez had a feeling that Easley was suspicious—he was jumpy working around the plane. Different scenarios ran through Montez' mind. Things that could go wrong: maybe Easley wouldn't go to the village; maybe there'd be a surprise witness, even a gun.

"Hey, Montez." Morelli yelled. "You've been staring into that wheel well for a half-hour. Thinking about those broads waiting for you in Frisco?"

"No gals will be waiting for a pug-ugly like you when you get there," Montez replied.

Morelli gave him the Italian salute and continued the struggle with a recalcitrant auxiliary power unit in the rear of the plane. Montez tried to recapture the euphoria he usually felt in the early morning, but his mind turned back to Easley.

Montez felt that Easley didn't plan to kill Shelby, he just wanted to have a little fun, seriously scare him. But Easley's hatred or his fear, still caused Shelby's death, and Montez figured he had to pay for it. People like Easley couldn't be allowed to hurt others just because they were different.

Suddenly it struck him. He was trying to justify his own decision to kill Easley. He realized he was really remembering the fights he was pushed into as a kid — the ethnic taunting in his town. Easley deserved to get as good as he gave. And he was the one that had to do it.

They worked longer that day than Montez expected. He got back to the barracks when the sun hung low in the sky; and after a quick shower, he put on an old washed-out uniform. He had to get out of there fast to avoid Sol.

He jogged to the main gate, enjoying the blue and violet wildflowers that followed the road. He felt unusually aware of everything — the sky, the heavy, moist air, the road. His running feet raised small clouds of fine dirt.

Jose was waiting at the gate. "Big no-good sergeant just left."

"Was he alone?"

"He alone. You still leave for States?" He asked, hope in his voice.

"I'm leaving in four days unless something happens to change things. I don't think anything will."

Montez sat back on the hard cab seat and gazed beyond the dusty road's edge to the beginning of the shiny deep-green Okinawan holly and pine trees. In the foliage were wild hibiscus bushes displaying brilliant red flowers. Mariko used hibiscus flowers to brew soothing teas and even for laying on spells — she admitted she had used a magic potion to make Shelby love her. She also admitted that she felt ashamed that it took a potion to catch him. Montez tried to change her mind about the magical potion and felt he succeeded a little.

He tried to clear his mind of all irrelevant thoughts and focused on his driver's muscular back and pumping legs. "My friend, it may be tonight." He waited for some comment. "Drop me off before you normally do. And take off — I don't want you involved."

Jose peddled the bicycle stoically. "I tell you, I stay." Montez opened his mouth to repeat his warning and then decided it would be futile.

"Okay. But I don't want you too close to me. You understand? I need to surprise him."

"No sweat. I not be in way. I hide, take you back to base after you kick ass."

The ride to Easley's house seemed shorter than usual. Montez wondered if his nervous movements were obvious to Jose. He started deep breathing techniques taught by Mr. Ito and forced himself to relax.

Mr. Ito had taught him kyusho-jitsu, the art of pressure-point fighting. He knew this was taught only to advanced students who demonstrated the appropriate levels of skill, responsibility and character. According to Mr. Ito, Montez sure as hell didn't have them. Yet, after he understood Montez' mission, he taught him, anyway.

Mr. Ito's instructions ran through his mind: a closed fist striking pressure points in the nervous system will kill if thrown in full power; if one misses the pressure point, it will still do severe damage and temporarily disable the opponent. His voice resonated in Montez' mind. Employ redirection, stay balanced, use the entire body when executing a technique. He had bruises from Mr. Ito's punishing throws and light strikes when he didn't pay the appropriate attention. But tonight Montez felt he was ready.

"Jose, it's going to be a fine night to render to one that which is his due. Did a Roman emperor say something like that?"

"Don't know, Boss."

"Name's Juan, damn it."

The driver turned to Montez with a toothy smile, "Okay, Juan-boss."

Montez gazed at the bright Okinawan moon. Dusk had quickly turned into a clear night, and he would be able to clearly see Easley's face. He suddenly thought that he would have to hit Easley fast and hard — he might have a weapon.

One mile from Easley's house, they passed a village perched on high ground. Coming down the incline, Montez was surprised to see a pedicab off the road. Jose slowed down. Just as they were about to pass, Easley stepped out. He had a sneer on his face and a bottle of Nippon in his hand. Montez jumped off the cab and motioned for Jose to leave.

"I knew it was you following me," Easley said, derision raising his high-pitched voice. "You son of a bitch, want trouble? I'll smear yore greaser ass all over the ground."

Montez checked out the surroundings. Small rocks, no wood lying around to use as a weapon, and a slight incline to the right. The beer bottle could do some real damage, he thought as he slowly circled the heavier man.

"Well, come on you fucking chicken shit," Easley motioned Montez forward with his left arm. "You peeing in yore pants now, you goddamned wetback?"

Continuing his slow circle around Easley, Montez waited patiently for his move. He'd lost the element of surprise, but he wasn't nervous. He could see that Easley grew more agitated with every passing second. He saw Easley's arm rise, the bottle in the right hand. He came at Montez, as if in slow motion. Montez dodged to his left keeping his balance, hearing the bottle swish pass his right ear and hit his right shoulder a glancing blow.

Easley's rush was expected. Montez raised his right arm, his fist tight, and let Easley's face smash into it. His circular leg motion hit the side of Easley's leg hard enough to feel it give out under him. Easley fell sideways. Montez instantly crouched and then felt the pain in his right shoulder where Easley had hit him.

"You son of a bitch! " Easley bellowed as he tried to get up. "You broke my nose. I'm going to kill you."

Montez decided to let him get up. He could have quickly dispatched him when he was floundering on the ground, but suddenly he knew he couldn't kill him.

"I was going to do to you what you did to Shelby." He spit out, "I wanted to be sure you'd die slowly... and in pain." He slowly edged around Easley, watching the other man's feet. "But I changed my mind. You aren't worth killing."

Easley staggered to his feet, blood gushing from his broken nose. He reached for Montez. Slipping under groping hands, Montez hit him at a point near his ear and jaw, and then struck his mouth, twice. Pivoting his body away from Easley, he rammed his foot hard into Easley's ribs and then again at Easley's knee cap toppling him sideways like a sack of potatoes. He felt his ribs crack and knew he damaged his leg badly.

"I didn't mean to kill him." Easley screamed through the blood on his face. "I tried to stop

Whitey from hitting him so many times. You broke my leg, you bastard. I tried to stop...."

Montez stifled an urge to hit him again. "You're a lucky bastard. While you heal, I hope you think of what you did to Shelby and his family. He didn't have a chance to heal."

He spun and staggered to the top of the hill to find Jose. He felt light-headed, euphoric—as if he could leap high and touch the moon.

Easley's cab was gone, but Jose was there. He had seen it all and was so excited he tramped back and forth, his fist hitting his other palm.

"You very good, boss. You kill him?"

"Don't call me—never mind. No, I'm not very good. Sergeant very bad. He doesn't know how to fight, unless he has others to help him. As soon as we get out of here, you go get some help for the sergeant."

"No sweat. I take care everything. Maybe we have biru at restaurant?"

"Let's just get out of here. Go back to Kadena Air Base."

Montez listened to Jose's excited babble about the fight, and a strange lassitude crept through his body. He was relaxed, at peace with the world. He didn't want to think about Shelby, Easley or anyone else.

As they passed a village, Jose pulled up to a house, talked to a nodding mama-san. He came back with four large bottles of Nippon beer.

"Okay, everything taken care. Mama-san get help for sergeant. I buy biru for you and me."

"Here, I'll take care of those." Montez reached into his pocket, and a pain stabbed his right shoulder. Good thing that Easley hadn't connected on his face.

"No boss. I buy. Tonight very good night."

They parked the cab outside the village and Montez let Jose describe the fight in detail to him while he savored the fetid aroma of Okinawa and stared at the Okinawan sky dotted with huge bright stars. He knew this small passing of time would be imprinted on his mind forever. Tomorrow he would ask for Mariko's forgiveness for not fully avenging Shelby. Tonight he would spend time enjoying the moment. He wished Edwards, Sol, and Shelby could be drinking beer with him discussing today's events and their future in the States. Then he knew — he'd keep calling Edwards in Tennessee, or where ever he turned up, until he convinced him to come to California.

Jose broke into his musing, and Montez realized that a long period of time had quietly passed. "You think about leaving Okinawa, but you no happy like other GIs."

"You're right … and wrong, too," Montez replied thoughtfully. "I will miss Mariko and little Shelby-san, and you too. I'll even miss Okinawa, but I also want to go home."

"We miss you too, Boss. But, like GI say, maybe see you later, alligator. "

The following morning was not a good one. He dreaded saying goodbye to Mariko and Mr.

Ito—but today he had Sol as a buffer. After a skimpy breakfast of toast and coffee, they met Jose at the gate and told him to take it easy getting to Mariko's house. Sol didn't know about the fight, and he was going to tell him during their ride.

"Too bad you not at fight, Sol-san. Juan-boss beat shit out of sergeant."

Sol looked at Montez quizzically, "What is he talking about. You got into a fight?"

"I was going to tell you, but that loudmouth beat me to it."

Montez took a breath and quickly recounted the fight. "I didn't kill him. I only beat the hell out of him—left him just a little better off than they left Shelby."

He waited for the inevitable questions.

"How come you don't have any bruises or anything?" Sol queried. "How could you have done anything to that fat cochon without getting any marks on you?"

"I do have some marks, on my chest and my shoulder. Easley was more bark than bite, but I kept away from the reach of his arms and hands."

Sol peered at Montez' right hand. "I think you better have that hand looked at—it's swollen."

"Yeah, I'll have Morley look at it when we get back."

"You ought to have a doctor look at it," Sol insisted. "Morley's a good medic, but you might need X-rays."

"Okay. It does hurt. Just don't say anything about it to Mariko."

Mariko and Mr. Ito were waiting for them, talking about the flowers along the stone walkway in front of her house. Montez felt a twinge in the pit of his stomach — he'd helped her plant them only a few months ago, and he wouldn't be here again. He gazed about him, trying to imprint the house, walkway and the flowers in his mind, but gloom clouded his mind — this would be their last farewell.

Jose left, promising to return to pick them up. Montez understood. Jose knew this would be his last meeting with Mariko before he went home.

Mariko pulled Montez to the back of the house to see the small garden she just planted. "I don't want you be sad, Monty-san. I always think of you."

"Mariko, I want to tell you something. I didn't kill the man who killed Shelby-san. I couldn't do it." Montez added. "My duty to you and Shelby wasn't completed... I'm sorry."

"I knew you not kill bad man. You nice man." Mariko smiled at him. "I no want that you kill and Shelby-san no want."

A weight lifted off his shoulders. "I did hit the sergeant pretty hard. I think he will hurt for some time."

"Good. Now we go inside house." She tugged at him again, this time at his sore arm. He winced and she quickly dropped his arm.

"Come, we have tea. I fix arm and no hurt for awhile."

After tea, Mariko tended to his arm and shoulder with her homemade potions.

"It hurt? Sukoshi ne? She asked when he flinched.

"Hurt a little bit. No problem."

He knew he would have to see a doctor when she told him that something might be broken in his hand and wrist.

Mr. Ito waited patiently to talk to him alone. After awhile, Montez excused himself. "Sol, I'm going to Mr. Ito's house, I left some gear there."

He started to tell Mr. Ito about the fight before they reached his house, but Mr. Ito put up his hand for him to wait. They went into his house and the old man indicated for him to sit on a mat. With great ceremony, he poured sake into two small fine cups, bowed, then sat down to hear the story.

Montez had to tell him the lay of the land, every step he took, even his breathing. Mr. Ito had him repeat certain movements, making sucking sounds as he listened. Montez wondered if they indicated approval or dissatisfaction. Finally, after three cups of sake, Mr. Ito was satisfied.

"I tell you as your teacher on your action. You did poorly when he strike you with bottle. Only untrained would allow body to be hit with weapon." Mr. Ito thought for a while and then went on. "You use self-defense skill in real battle.

Very different from training in dojo. You use efficient strikes in battle; don't use full power. Very good." Montez took a deep breath and began to feel better.

"You did very well at times. You made him come to you. He was off-balance so at your will." Montez's growing relief was quickly squashed.

"You continue karate in States. Maybe five years, you okay in basic techniques. Perhaps be better in redirection and parrying—you need."

Mr. Ito got to his feet, walked to a corner of the training hall and returned with a deep purple sash and a heavy off-white kimono. He bowed and presented them to Montez. "You train hard. Perhaps earn honor. You have talent and desire."

Montez quickly got to his feet, bowed and accepted the present. "I will work very hard to make you proud of me." His spirits lifted with pride—he received a great honor from a karate master

They walked back to Mariko's house and spent the next few hours remembering Shelby and laughing over Edwards' antics. Mariko touched Montez's arm, "Monty-san, please, you walk outside with me."

They slowly walked around the small village chatting and admiring the varied flowers at every neighbor's yard, an old present from Shelby, until Mariko stopped, "I want to go Stateside because of the baby. I think about what you say. Better for little Shelby-san in States; he has you, Sol-san, and Edwards-san. I go."

"I'm very happy you made up your mind. You talk to your lawyer in Naha—he has been waiting for your call," Montez added, somewhat sheepishly. "I told him you would call him soon... when you were ready. He will work with Boston lawyer. It may take some time, but you'll make it."

They walked back to her house in time for Jose's arrival. "Time to leave, Boss."

The last thing Montez remembered was a tearful Mariko imploring him to write every week.

As Jose pumped the pedals of the bicycle-cab, Montez looked back at the disappearing village with a lump in his throat. Jose took his time getting to the base knowing Montez was looking at scenery he would never see again. As they got close to the gates, Montez had Jose stop while he pulled out a roll of script and gave it to him. "Jose part of this money is a bonus for your help and the rest is for looking after Mariko. I know you said you would take care of her as much as possible and didn't ask for anything—so don't take it as an insult for your generosity." Jose stared at more money than he had ever seen in his life.

"Arigato, Boss, I understand. Sayonara, Boss-san."

As he trudged to the barracks, Montez thought that Shelby wouldn't mind using his money for a nice bonus to a friend. He picked up his pace, felt much better about leaving and hardly felt any pain in his shoulder or hand.

❖ ❖ ❖ ❖ ❖

Watching the churning white wake of the liberty ship gave Montez a sense of peace. He didn't know if he was happy to be going home or sad because he was leaving. He leaned over the cold metal rail as far as he could, favoring a small cast on his right hand and wrist, then rocking back, took deep breaths of the wet air. He wasn't seasick, but the thumping ship's engines through the metal deck gave him a headache. For hours, he stared down at the dark blue ocean. Maybe it didn't make any difference. He'd be discharged in a couple of months, starting a new life. He might as well make the best of it. He would see Sol this summer and, who knows, that crazy Edwards might just show up—wouldn't that be something.

Tokyo was a disappointment. He couldn't find Michiko, so he cruised the streets with a couple of airmen from a B-29 crew stationed in Japan. They wanted to booze it up before they went home, and he wanted to see the sights before the ship left. He left them after the first day and spent his remaining time visiting temples and a kabuki theatre, which reminded him of Michiko.

The Air Force drew guard duty on the ship this time, and Army personnel were assigned kitchen police. Montez hated KP, but guarding the hundreds of caskets of slain military in the ship's hold was spooky. Thumping sounds came from the hold at night as if the corpses were trying to get out.

The third day at sea, Montez was leaning on the railing at the bow of the ship, upwind of sick soldiers, when he heard his name called by an airman who had been stationed at Kadena Airbase.

"Wasn't the assistant crew chief on your plane Sergeant Easley?"

"Yeah," Montez answered, his body instantly alert.

"There's something on him in the Ryukyu Review; you know — the local paper. Take a look."

The airman handed him the paper and rejoined his friends playing poker. Montez unfolded the newspaper, afraid of what he would find.

It was a small article at the bottom of the second page:

Kadena AFB, Okinawa. December 1. Sergeant Wilber Easley, stationed at Kadena AFB, was hospitalized yesterday after an Okinawan woman found him by the roadside near her village. According to Doctor Maurice Savio, Easley sustained a fractured leg, broken ribs and nose, and a dislocated jaw. The Sergeant said he was beaten by two Marines who jumped him. The reason for the attack was unclear. An investigation is underway.

Montez stared at the newspaper, and then carefully folded it in half. He made no attempt to stop grinning. Shaking his head, he turned again toward the sea.

Damn if he didn't join the Marines after all.

Made in the USA
Charleston, SC
06 November 2016